YpHi

YpHi

Graham Moyson

YpHi

Text copyright©2023 Graham Moyson
Cover image copyright©2023 Katherine Mabey

ISBN 978-1-7393239-0-5

British Library Cataloguing in Publication Data.
A catalogue record for this book is available from the
British Library.

3 5 4 2 1

First Published in Great Britain
Hawkwood Books 2023

Printed and bound in Great Britain by CPI Group (UK)
Ltd. Croydon CR0 4YY

CONTENTS

0000 0001: WHEN DREAMS COME TRUE

Moving hadn't been the positive change her mother had promised. Dilly, not so long ago, thought she had friends for life, but here she was, at thirteen, unexpectedly friendless and frighteningly alone. She'd said goodbye to everything and everyone she knew, Abi especially. They promised to keep in touch and absolutely meant to, but London was light years from their dusty, blustery home by the sea. Dilly had not wanted this move but her mother was mad keen. It was an 'opportunity not to be missed'. She'd spent years in various jobs from offices to supermarkets, struggling to keep heads above water, always aware of the artist imprisoned in her heart. Out of the blue, this magical thing had happened. Pennies from heaven. Many pennies. Countless pennies. Could she turn down this once in a lifetime chance? They would go to London, to this new glass wonderland, where Art thrived, and it would work out. Wait and see.

Three manic weeks had passed in which Abi was fast becoming a virtual friend and their lives had changed from routine to a frenzy of disorienting sounds and daunting sights. Mum was busy setting up "Dilly Enterprises" in her fabulous new studio in the biggest room of their brand spanking new apartment, but for Dilly, not a new friend on the horizon. It was the summer holidays, no school yet, no chance to meet 'girls and boys your own age'. No fairy tale girl living next door, just a hubbub of adults busy as ants.

So Dilly was alone. She helped where she could but her mother was working at the speed of light, determined to make the best use of their good fortune. Dilly saw how much her mother's work meant and did nothing to upset her, never a complaint, not once, but she was not a happy bunny. A dad would have been useful at this point, but she'd never known hers, gone with the wind. Maybe mum could find a replacement here, one of their neighbours in this glass monstrosity. Well, that was about as likely as them winning the lottery.

Except, they had won.

Five numbers had turned their lives upside down, back to front and inside out. Dilly would never forget the moment. Mum, staring at her her phone as if trying to decipher a foreign language.

"Dilly?"

Her name had hung in the air for a second that seemed like a lifetime.

"I've got five numbers."

That was it. Five numbers. You could see them on buses, on door numbers, on receipts for the smallest, silliest things, everywhere. They weren't special, but they'd come together in this crazy way to drop treasure on their doorstep, enough to uproot and move to the city paved with gold.

Now, Dilly wished that five other numbers had been selected. What was the point of such fortune if it didn't make you happy? And she wasn't happy, she was sure of that. She wasn't sure of many things, but knowing they had won the holy grail of prizes hadn't had the same effect on her as it had had on mum, that was clear. Mum seemed to have a ton weight lifted off her shoulders. Dilly had watched events in confusion, believing that everything would be better. Perhaps her AWOL dad would reappear and all would be well, but what kind of dad would he be to show his face for such a reason? Not a good one, she'd bet on that. Instead, various strangers popped up, mostly in suits, always happy. And why not? It was their job to impart good news in a world full of bad news, and they clearly enjoyed it. Had mum announced publicly what had happened, heaven knew how many other strangers would have turned up, crawling out of the woodwork to be part of the frenzy. She didn't, though, partly because she knew what would happen, and partly because it wasn't the kind of win that merited national attention. The pot of gold wasn't the size to let you buy entire islands or half a planet, it was just right for what mum wanted to do, to live in the greatest city of the world and be the artist she'd always ached to be. Dilly's mother was young enough to still have fire in her heart, ideas to express and bundles of energy. She wanted to see what London had to offer and to offer London whatever it was she had locked inside her for the best part of forever.

Dilly was lost in all the excitement and disturbing newness of it all. She was old enough to know the value the grown up world put on wealth, but not old enough to be thinking about it all day long. She was more aware of how lonely she felt, despite the excitement, the changes and, as mum kept saying, 'the possibilities'. It was as if some secret to happiness had been withheld from her. The unexpected windfall might have lessened some worries but had created others. And these, Dilly felt, she couldn't share because she didn't understand them and could do nothing about them. She might be surrounded by shiny new things on the top floor of a brand new tower block in the heart of the greatest city in the world (some said) but she felt a terrible emptiness, as if she'd been cast into space and all around was a vast, soulless void. She put on a brave show not to upset her mother, but inside but was sinking, almost falling, into an abyss of misery. Her mother, though, was not fooled.

"Darling Dilly," she said one evening after another day of buying, talking and getting to know their new home, "are you happy?"

"Yes, of course I am," she replied with as much conviction as possible. "It's just that…"

"You don't know anyone. I understand. When I was your age…" and mum went into a history of her own childhood which of course had been nothing like this. There were changes in everyone's lives, but rarely as sudden and as seismic. There was no way mum could convince her that this was something she'd been through herself. And anyway, they were different people. Family members often came out chalk and cheese. If Dilly had had a sister or brother, there'd be no telling how different they would be, but she didn't have either and could only imagine one, which she did, quite a lot.

"Once school begins," said mum, "you'll be surprised how quickly everything will fall into place. You'll have new friends, new experiences, a whole new everything." Dilly remained unconvinced. There hadn't been that much wrong with the old world. "Meanwhile," mum went on, "we've got the IT bods coming tomorrow, so make space in your room for them to work, darling. And help me get things ready."

In their old house, they'd had free TV with not a streaming service in site and painfully slow WiFi but this brand spanking new tower block apartment was rigged with state of the art electronics.

Did this excite Dilly? Not a lot. In fact, it daunted her. The thing that made her happiest was a good read in a quiet corner, untouched and untroubled. She'd read so much, it was already as if she'd led a hundred lives in histories that never happened, futures that would never happen, make believe adventures, secret gardens, wonderful dreams, impenetrable jungles, all with friends that she knew, even if they didn't know her. There was something so private, having these make believe memories all to yourself, where you could cheer on the good and jeer the wicked, where anything could happen, and often did. She assumed that her new school would have a library, but there were weeks to go before she could use it. London had a million bookshops, but she'd have to explore to find them, and mum wasn't too happy about letting her roam wild and free just yet. For the moment, she'd re-read some of the books she'd brought with her. It didn't hurt to revisit old friends who gave her comfort when the world around her was changing at a rate of knots.

She helped tidy and make space for whatever the IT bods had to do. This was not easy. They still had boxes piled up to the ceiling, more than they'd brought with. Mum had apparently ordered the whole online world, much of which remained in unopened packaging. How the engineers would work around all these was a mystery. Dilly held on to her books for dear life, as if the stories inside gave her courage to deal with this onslaught of change, and imagination to find her way through the tangled maze of her new life. She found a secluded corner in between three huge boxes and took out her phone. It was still the tacky old one she'd brought with. She might just as well have used tin cans and a piece of string.

"Abi?"

"Hello, Rich Girl."

Dilly's heart sank.

"I'm still 'Dill', still me"

Silence.

"So how are things?" Abi asked. "In Fairy Land?"

"Where dreams come true? I'm still dreaming."

"Not about us, I bet."

"About everything."

"Don't see what there is to dream about once dreams come true."

"It wasn't my dream, Abi."

"If you say so. You still left."

"I could hardly stay, could I? You know that." Another silence. They were more and more frequent whenever they spoke. "I miss you."

"Suppose I miss you, too."

"Suppose?"

"Yeh, well…"

"What's happening, Abi. There must be things happening."

"Must there?"

"You're my friend, Abi, don't be horrible. Tell me something."

Abi thought for a moment then reeled off a few gossipy things about all the people Dilly had left behind. Dilly tried to picture them all but it was surprisingly hard. The names were already receding into history and Abi sensed it. They did their best to laugh about things as they'd done since they were kids, but somehow it sounded hollow, or as if they were trying too hard. Dilly was desperate not to let Abi go, but Abi didn't seem the same.

"I could have kept it a secret," said Dilly, "we did, from the telly people. You're my best friend, that's why I told you."

"I know," said Abi, "and I haven't told anyone. Except…"

"Except?"

"No one, honestly, but people aren't stupid. They say things."

"Like what?"

"All kinds of things. You can't hide what happened, Dill."

Dilly knew this. Mum wanted to tell the world, at first, she was so excited. When she changed her mind, the telly people were fine about it, but it was truly an impossible thing to hide from everyone. It was like a ripple in a pond that spread out and out until it faded away, but unlike the watery ripples, gossipy ones left jealous whispers behind.

"Has anyone guessed?"

"How do I know?" Abi answered. "Probably."

"I don't care," said Dilly. "They can say what they like. I'm still me."

"Not exactly," said Abi. Dilly asked what she meant. "You can't still be the exact same you. It's not possible."

"Don't see why not."

"You mean you don't want to see why not. It's obvious. You're not here, you're there, in some big, shiny expensive new home with all new friends..."

"I don't have friends here."

"Yet," said Abi. "They won't be like me and the others. They won't at all. They'll all be posh."

Dilly didn't know whether to laugh or cry. 'Posh' was a silly word, the wrong word. Dilly hadn't moved into Buckingham Palace or shared a room with a princess.

"You think I won't want to talk to you?"

"Maybe."

"That's not how I want it to be."

"If you say so," said Abi.

"It's crazy here," said Dilly, trying to interest her old friend and play down the sparkle of it all. "They haven't finished building so there's always noise."

Abi asked what was there before but Dilly didn't know for sure. It was hard enough working out where she was now, let alone thinking about its history. Yet there had been people there - many, if the scraps of talk she'd heard meant anything.

"You can visit," said Dilly, "see it for yourself."

Abi didn't answer straight away, which said a lot in itself.

"Maybe. Depends, doesn't it. You're a long way away."

"I am," said Dilly. "It would be nice to see you."

"Yep," said Abi, half-heartedly.

Dilly felt miserable. Was Abi just jealous? If it all had happened the other way around, would Dilly be jealous? She hoped not, but she wasn't sure. Why else would Abi be so grudging? And then it occurred to her that Abi might be as unhappy as her. After all, she'd lost her best friend, too. It wasn't easy to stay close when you were hundreds of miles away from each other.

"I'd better go," said Dilly. "We've got someone coming tomorrow to get our TV and WiFi going. I'm supposed to be making space. It's a mess."

"I'm sorry," said Abi.

"For what?" Dilly asked. "Me having to tidy up?"

"No. For me being bitchy."

"That's alright."

"It isn't really, Dill. And I don't see how it can be. Ever."

When the call ended, Dilly stared at the old phone as if it was its fault that Abi had been so ungenerous. Mum had warned her, people being people, but Dilly didn't want to believe it of her best friend. Like she thought, Abi was probably as upset as she was envious, maybe more so. Mum had also said that if friends took that attitude, then perhaps they weren't friends at all, which was not much comfort. They'd been together so long, it would be hard if not impossible to find someone as close.

She leaned on the window sill of her cluttered new bedroom. She stared outside at the panorama, almost as if it were a different planet. It might as well have been. Nothing in the landscape looked familiar. There was hardly a space to be seen amongst the rising blocks of concrete and glass. Maybe a patch of green here and there but this was a vast, ambitious project, one that would take years to finish. Surely mum could have found somewhere done and dusted, where there were no diggers, lorries or cranes in every direction. True, the windows were so over-glazed that not a sound came through, but Dilly loved the sounds of nature, of birds, even of nothing, just life happening in its own sweet way. There was nothing sweet about this unnatural vacuum. It was a daunting crystal jungle built by those with a futuristic view of how people should live, as if they were modelling their creation on a comic or some daft science fiction film. And how high would the buildings go around her, Dilly wondered. She could at least see a panorama of London, which was some consolation, but if the adjacent buildings kept growing, this would become a nightmare. All light would be blocked out, the panorama would vanish, she would be closed in as if in prison, albeit with comfy sofas, a spaceship kitchen and a huge TV. Mum didn't know and didn't seem to care. She said she would ask, but as the structures around them were still at ground level, they wouldn't become beanstalk buildings overnight.

Dilly opened a window and the world changed for a few moments. It wouldn't open wide, but enough to let a little air in and the sounds of men and women at work. They had a balcony, but that was only accessible from the front room, not her bedroom. Here, her only vivid take on the world was through a narrow gap between the open window and the white concrete wall. She sniffed the air, remembering the sea breeze of what once had been home. It was cold and different, but bits of dust clung to the air, floating up from below as if desperate to shake off their own natures.

She looked down. It was dizzying to see the ground so far below with people appearing small and fragile. There was a kind of beauty there, she accepted that, but it was a distant, unreal beauty. She preferred the close up, undeniable beauty of a petal, a leaf or a water droplet. This was something alien and she did not know if she would ever get used to it, or even if she wanted to get used to it. Abi could not be jealous if she were up here, now, seeing and feeling what Dilly saw and felt.

She could see nothing of what had been there before, apart from rapidly disappearing piles of red bricks. Men had done what they always do, created and destroyed. Creation took an age, destruction a moment. Whatever had been there was now a memory in someone else's history, not hers, perhaps pictures in books or photos she might search for on the internet when it was all up and running. She didn't feel like it then. It would make her sad to see it because there was no way it could be worse than this. If there had had been young people there, her age, they would not have been locked away like Rapunzel in this high castle. She'd seen clips of times past but they merged together into something called 'history'. She couldn't tell one year from another, not even one decade from another. Those days were gone and forgotten, but Dilly wondered whether it might have been Paradise compared to this silvery prison in the sky.

0000 0010: WiFi

The engineer was from a company called Aural Communications, a friendly man of an age that Dilly couldn't guess. 'Adult' covered a multitude of sins. He didn't look as though he could sin at all, this man with eyes that reflected a captivating sparkle. Dilly's mother followed him around, keeping an eye on the work but also on him, despite the wedding ring on his left hand.

"We've tidied it as best we can," she said.

"Oh, don't worry about the boxes," he replied. "You should see some of the places I have to wire up. Nightmare. Shouldn't take long, though."

They watched him work, fascinated.

"It is the best, isn't it?" mum asked.

He laughed and said, "Best money can buy. Fast as lightning. You'll be getting stuff delivered before you order it."

She smiled, then asked provocatively, "I take it the wedding ring is current?"

Dilly blushed.

"Best wife in the world and best daughter, too."

"Shame," answered Dilly's mother. Dilly looked up to heaven.

He tested the connections and devices in each room. Everything worked fine. When it was done and dusted, he said, "Your free gift," and handed Dilly a brand spanking new mobile phone. "We offer this with new installations. Special ones, at least," he added.

"Mine?" Dilly asked.

"Yours," he said.

The mobile was a gentle shade of green, her favourite

colour, along with the rest of the world. Big screen, quite light in weight, state of the art. It felt right in her hands, which not all mobiles did. Dilly thanked him.

"You're welcome," he replied. "Use it well," which was a strange thing to say, but said with his usual charm. "You won't have to leave this comfortable home ever," he said, looking around. "Solid as stone, this system. Be happy, that's the important thing. It isn't easy, moving, my family know that. We've moved around a fair bit. But you'll be alright, I know it. And don't be afraid of this technology, it's there to serve, like me."

"Dilly will help me out if I get stuck, won't you, Dill?"

Dilly nodded, still staring at the phone. Did they really give free mobiles at each installation. Special ones? What was special with theirs?

When they were alone, mum repeated, "Be happy, Dilly. You heard the man."

Dilly's mother sent to work on her desktop while Dilly setup her new mobile. There were, as ever, a whole list of WiFi connections, all of them familiarly anonymous and unimaginative. The tower block was apparently full of bright sparks with little interest in colourful WiFi names.

Except for one.

Hidden away near the bottom of the list was:

YpHi711172123275

It didn't trip lightly off the tongue or stay in memory but it was different, and faintly familiar. It glowed pink. Dilly stared at it and tapped it, but nothing happened. When she scrolled up and back, it had gone. She hoped the new phone wasn't faulty.

"Dill," her mother called, popping her head in at the door, "duty calls. Shop or starve."

They shopped together, a decision they'd made until they got to know the neighbourhood better. The supermarket was nestled in amongst the scaffold and bricks of the new build homes. It was a local version of a brand which had super and hyper versions throughout the country, but local was all they needed. The staff were immaculate, as were the aisles, the tills and the shelves. Dilly looked around to see if there was anyone her age. No one. The shoppers were mainly young men and women who looked as locked up as she felt. Was there really a school with hundreds of students?

"Mum, do you mind if I wait outside?" she asked.

Dilly could hardly breathe in there. She hurried out and stood for a while, taking in the sights and sounds of her new home. It wasn't Narnia, but it was a strange, new country. In the few weeks she'd been there, it still hadn't taken shape in her head. There was so much going on and so much changing all the time. Brick by brick, stone by stone, pane of glass by pane of glass, the new – what should she call it because it was not home – rose from the rubble of what had been there before. Some things were finished, like their tower. You could not live in a roofless tower block. The gym was finished, though, which said a lot about priorities. There it was, gleaming and showy with its massive glass front into which you could see dozens of bizarre machines like a warped vision of the future, except that this was now. Most of them were empty, possibly because only a few people had moved in, so far. Dilly and her mum were amongst the first.

What would Abi think if she saw this? Would she still be envious? Surely not. How could anyone? Dilly thought of taking photos with her new mobile, enticing Abi to visit, but changed her mind. She suspected that Abi would not visit for a long time, maybe not ever. There was, surprisingly, a boating lake, but Dilly had no idea how to make use of it. It was for grown ups with boats of their own. You couldn't see it from there, in front of the supermarket, but it was a ten minute walk away. Other than that, there was little greenery, except for a couple of painted waste bins. No trees, and just some humble flower beds, about as unwild as a picnic in a park.

Dilly sat on the little wall surrounding one of the flower beds. She took out her new phone and examined it. Most phones looked similar but this was slightly different – or was it her imagination? The green was a unique shade, one that Dilly couldn't place in nature. The casing was textured and easy to handle, almost melting into her palm. It was also surprisingly warm, despite the weather being a typically British summer's day, cool and cloudy. There was just one bar showing on the network connection which was a surprise, considering that this was the centre of one of the greatest cities in the world.

Another surprise was that a WiFi signal appeared. She shouldn't have had a connection at all. Their home system was way out of range and others were security protected. She scrolled to the WiFi settings and saw another list of unknown names, some obviously from the supermarket, others from places close by. But there, all lit up was

YpHi711172123275

the ridiculously long one she'd seen at home. Whatever it was, it shouldn't be seen here – wherever the router was, it had to be too far away to show up. Very strange. And it was glowing bold and red, no loner pale pink. Was there a bug in her phone? Drat.

A box appeared with an instruction beneath: 'Tap to connect'

Curiouser and curiouser, she said to herself, quoting one of her favourite characters. What would Alice have made of this? Mobile phones were complicated things and could go wrong, just like any machine, but this didn't feel wrong – it felt odd. You needed a password for WiFi. You needed a password to breathe in the twenty-first century. Everything was kept safe and secure – until someone hacked it to pieces. What was the point of a WiFi with no password? And why was it red?

And now it was flashing!

As her finger hovered over the name, Dilly hesitated. She didn't know why she did, but she did. The phone felt even warmer in her hand, not just normal warmth, but noticeable heat. Was it overheating? Maybe that was causing it to malfunction. She put it down on the brick wall beside her. The red instruction faded to orange, then yellow, then white. Dilly's eyes opened wide. She picked it up and the colour changed from white through yellow to orange then red.

She told herself not to be silly. Science explained everything, eventually, and this could be explained. She would take it somewhere in the morning and ask, or just Google it. The phone probably had a sensor inside the case which responded to hand heat. And yet it did not feel like a normal response. There was something different about this. It didn't feel like part of the normal operation. Nothing had flashed red and and bold before. It felt like an SOS, an emergency signal, but of course it could not be.

Dilly clasped the phone tightly, her finger hovering over the screen like the sword of Damocles.

"Don't be a baby," she said to herself, "it's an error in the software, a glitch. Tap it and see, silly."

She readied her finger and was about to touch the screen when, "Dilly!" Her mother was signalling to her at the door of the supermarket. "You're miles away. Come and help me carry these." Dilly put the phone in her pocket and took two bags from her mother. "These phones," said her mum, "it's a wonder you youngsters don't get your noses stuck to them."

"What about you," said Dilly, "it's your best friend.

Besides…"

"Besides what," mum asked when Dilly hesitated.

"Oh… erm… nothing."

When they arrived home, Dilly took out the phone and checked the WiFi networks. She scrolled up and down, her eyes ready for the red flashing signal. Nothing. Their own network showed up, as it should, and the others she'd seen before, but the mysterious one was no longer there. It wasn't as if it had changed back to to white, it simply was not there.

The next day, Dilly found some excuse to return to the supermarket alone. Her mind was on her misbehaving new mobile, an itch that couldn't be scratched. On the wall by the supermarket, she sat, took out the phone and looked again, full of expectation. Nothing. 'Drat and double drat,' she whispered to herself. She spent ten minutes scrolling up and down, changing the settings, turning the phone off and on – which is what IT bods told the world to do for every problem – and Googling 'red WiFi' and 'bold WiFi'. Google didn't have a clue.

Two weeks went by but the 'glitch' in the phone never reappeared. That was all it was. Glitches happened with every human invented machine and it fell away from from her mind as something far more important approached – the first day at her new school, a comprehensive, a short bus ride away. She and mum had visited it so she knew what to expect, but with six hundred children, a lot of staff and pressure on every one to do better than anyone else, Dilly was anxious. She hoped she wouldn't stand out for any reason. Mum had wished her well but Abi hadn't called. That saddened her. It wouldn't have hurt Abi to wish Dilly luck.

She stood in the playground, new uniform pressed and spotless, hoping there would be someone, somewhere in all this mass of children who loved books and was on her wavelength. She wasn't confident. They all looked terribly smart and, well, posh. All uniforms were equal, that was the ideal, but some were more equal than others. So it seemed. There were little touches that made certain styles stand out. Dilly had never felt so alone and nervous. She'd missed the first years so all the girls would know each other whilst none of them would know her. She would be an outsider. The thing to do was merge in slowly, she told herself, not to make a fuss or a scene, just be as quiet as a church mouse and blend in gradually.

She sat on a bench and took out her phone. It might be collected as soon as school began, she wasn't sure, but for now it was her refuge.

The first thing she saw was the YpHi connection with its long string of unmemorable numbers after it, glowing red and bold and asking to be tapped. Dilly forgot she was in a playground surrounded by hundreds of new faces, focused completely on this bizarre message. She was miles from home, miles from wherever this WiFi signal originated. It should not be there, could not be there and must not be there, if science had any meaning, but there it was. She blinked.

This time, she did not hesitate. The message was clear, and clearly it was a message for her.

She tapped it.

0000 0011: LOST TIME

"Are you alright, love?"

Dilly opened her eyes to the shock of being surrounded by almost every child in the playground and three teachers, or at least three adults. Obviously, her gentle blending in idea was not going to work.

"What happened?" she whispered. "Where's Simon?"

She felt rather than heard the buzz of confusion.

"You fainted," said one of the adults, kneeling down beside her. "Let's get you up."

"But Simon," Dilly repeated. "Is he alright?"

Two of the adults lifted her onto the bench. The others ordered the circus of children all around to disperse and give her air.

"Let me stay, Miss Roberts," said a soft voice. "She'll need a friend."

The teacher touched the head of the girl who'd spoken, a gentle girl, herself new to the school, with a reputation that was hard to pin down.

"Alright, Laura. Now – Dilly, isn't it? Don't move too quickly. Take a deep breath."

Her head was spinning, but not just with the surprise of having the school stare at her like this. She knew beyond the shadow of a doubt that something remarkable had happened. That she had been somewhere, seen something, met someone – Simon, wasn't it? – and yet even as she tried to hold on to the memory, it receded, like sand running though her fingers. She was suddenly very scared. Clearly, she was not in danger here, but this, whatever 'this' was, shook her. She squeezed the little hand that held her own, if only to prove that at least something was real. The hand squeezed hers.

"This is Laura," said Miss Roberts. "She'll stay with you till you feel better. Can you stand up, Dilly? Don't if you feel wobbly."

She stood, sensing hundreds of eyes sizing her up. What kind of girl faints in the school playground for no reason? She could almost read their thoughts. She would be labelled weird straight away, and once you were labelled, nothing on Earth would change the way others saw you. But she could do nothing about it. Here she was, the unwanted centre of attention in the very place she'd wanted to be invisible.

Laura was smaller than Dilly with a kind face and calming touch. She was concerned, which itself was remarkable. Others seemed intrigued, but Laura was all there, after barely a minute.

"Make space," said Miss Roberts. "Good girl. Come on."

She and Laura led Dilly into the school building, every pair of eyes following them every step of the way, maybe waiting for her to fall again, or to discover some clue about what had happened. Inside, she was taken to the medical room and sat down.

"Laura, glass of water, please."

While Laura ran the tap, another adult poked her head around the door.

"Sam's been called, Irene."

Miss Roberts nodded. It was always impressive how news spread. Within a few minutes, the entire staff had heard that a new pupil had fainted in the playground. Some were even making jokes about it. 'Are we that scary?' 'Is school that bad?' 'Did she see the Head?'

Miss Roberts pulled up a chair in front of Dilly and let her sip the water. Laura watched on. Oddly, they all accepted her presence and no one asked her to leave.

"Is there something we should know about you?" Miss Roberts asked. "Are you diabetic? Any kind of medical condition? Your Head of House should have been told."

"No," said Dilly, "nothing. I don't know what happened."

"Has it happened before?"

"No. Never."

"Alright. Well don't worry. Laura and I will stay with you. We'll call your parents…"

"Just mum. Dad's… No dad," she said.

Laura squeezed her hand again.

Dilly wanted desperately to tell them what was going on inside her head, but she said nothing. What could she say? It would seem to all of them like she was, well, crazy. Maybe she was. She'd had dreams, everyone had dreams, but this one had been vivid. She would have sworn on her mother's life that it had happened. For all she knew, this room, with a strange girl holding her hand and an unknown lady talking to her – this was the dream. When she'd opened her eyes, she believed that was the case, that she was dreaming and that Simon was the reality. She even heard him calling – 'Stay. Please, don't go.'

She shook her head.

Was she ill? Was there something wrong with her that she didn't know about? Was she dying, maybe? Poor mum! Mum would scream the world down if Dilly died. No, she wasn't ill. She knew it. Her body felt strong and her mind was her own. The room came into focus and she gazed uncertainly at Laura and Miss Roberts.

"I feel alright now, really. I should start school properly now."

"Not yet," said Miss Roberts. "You sit still. You've got years of schooling ahead, it can wait a little while longer."

The door opened and an older woman came in. Miss Roberts stood and gestured to Dilly.

"Ah, yes," said the woman. "The fainter. Let's see now."

"This is Sam," Miss Roberts reassured Dilly, "our go-to guru for all things medical."

Sam looked into Dilly's eyes, felt her pulse and asked a few pertinent questions, name, address, age, illnesses and so on. She turned to Laura and said, "You are?"

"Laura. I need to keep her company. She's new, miss."

"New. Yes. That's kind, Laura. Alright. You seem like a sensible girl but I have to speak with her alone. Why don't you join your class and you can catch up with Dilly later."

"Will she be alright?"

"I think so. Don't you? Of course you do."

"Can she stay?"

They all looked at Dilly who'd asked the question without knowing that she was going to ask it. Laura had the look of someone older than her years and Dilly took to her immediately. After what had happened, she needed a friend.

"I'm afraid not," said Sam. "We've called your mother. She'll be here soon and we'll get you to the hospital."

Dilly looked startled and grabbed Laura's hand.

"Don't worry," said Sam, "it's a precaution. Alright, Laura, stay until Dilly's mum arrives. Let's get Dilly a drink, shall we?"

They gave her a tea and biscuits, keeping an eye on her the whole time, worried that the same thing might happen again. Sam, being medically minded, went through a hundred possibilities, but nothing was obvious.

"You asked for Simon," she said. "Is he your brother? A friend?"

Dilly looked embarrassed.

"He's... someone I met. I don't have any brothers or sisters."

"Well, he must be close to you. His was the name you

called first."

"Was it?" Dilly said. "Oh."

She seemed as if she was trying to hide something but neither Miss Roberts nor Sam wanted to push.

"It could be personal," said Laura, and the adults almost laughed. It was said with such innocence.

"Yes, I daresay it could be. Is the tea helping, Dilly?"

The tea was working wonders but not such wonders that it removed the memory of what had happened. She wanted to share it, to tell them, but if she did, she knew what they would think. She did not know what to think herself. She tried telling herself that it had been a dream, that the mind played tricks, and this was a particularly good one.

But she could not.

Whatever happened was as real as it was possible for reality to be. If she doubted it, then she would doubt herself, and she dare not do that. There would, however, be no point in explaining anything more. She would be digging a hole for herself too deep to escape.

"I'm sorry," Dilly said, "I can't tell you anything else. I'm a bit tired, that's all. I didn't mean to worry you. I'm fine now."

"You are a mystery," said Sam. "You're looking better but we must check this out. Don't be upset, if nothing's wrong, you'll be home before you can say Jack Robinson."

"Who?"

Sam laughed.

"Doesn't matter. Just an expression. Ah, here is your mother, I believe."

Mum almost burst in, tears in her eyes.

"Dilly! Whatever happened?"

Laura moved away to let Dilly's mum sit down. She watched, eyes wide open, absolutely glued to the scene, exuding both calm and concern.

"I'm alright," said Dilly, "I just… fainted, I think."

Sam explained what happened as Dilly's mum clung to her daughter, not knowing what to make of such a sudden and unexpected turn of events.

It was decided that Miss Roberts would take them to the hospital rather than call an ambulance. Dilly's mother looked too flustered to drive and was glad of the teacher's company. Laura wanted to go, too, but seeing as though she and Dilly had only been best friends for thirty minutes, she was left behind looking on in the kind of agony that made both Miss Roberts and Sam glad they'd chosen to be teachers.

"She'll be back soon enough," said Sam to Laura.

"She was hiding something," said Laura, "didn't you think so?"

Out of the mouth of babes, Sam thought.

"What was she hiding?" she asked.

Laura shook her head.

"Something she thought you wouldn't believe."

"My," said Sam, "you are the wise one. Listen, when she gets back, will you make sure she's okay, show her the ropes? You know, where the classes are, timetables, that sort of thing. Your new, too, I know, so you'll have that in common. Maybe that's what happened. The stress was too much for her."

"I don't think so, miss," said Laura, and once again, Sam wondered whether she was talking to a child or a psychotherapist.

"You don't?"

"I'll find out," said Laura, and Sam believed it.

Dilly's mum, meanwhile, had gathered her thoughts, but not her composure. Not totally, She asked Miss Roberts a dozen questions as she cradled Dilly in the back of the car. When they reached the hospital, they went to A&E and were met by a nurse who was expecting them. Now that never happened in real life, thought Dilly's mother, even though this was most definitely real. She realised that the school had called ahead, but as reassuring as it should have been, it also made her worry.

"You must think it's worse that you say," she said to Miss Roberts.

"Not at all," the teacher replied. "Better safe than sorry. Precaution, only. And now you're in safe hands, I have to return. What a first day, eh Dilly?"

Dilly smiled as best she could. It was a bit of a roller coaster, to say the least. Was it a day? How could it be, after all that had happened, after all she thought had happened?

"Dill?" said her mother, answer the doctor.

Dilly blinked. She'd dreamed away a few moments between Miss Roberts leaving and a doctor coming to speak with her. So many people!

"Sorry?" she said.

He asked her again to repeat what had happened and she told him all she could, all except the truth. That was impossible. Once more, if she did, they would say she was doolally and lock her away. She told him the basic facts as her mum held her hand, trying to be strong.

"Let me take a look," said the doctor, "Open your eyes wide. Look into this light. Let me see…"

Dilly wondered if the light would shine on the truth, on what she was hiding, but the doctor didn't seem to register shock. He said, "We will take a scan, Dilly, to make sure. Honestly, I can't see anything, but an MRI will show up any problems."

"What kind of problems?" Dilly's mother asked, fearful of terrible news.

"Hopefully none," said the doctor, "but we'll do it right away. They're very busy but Dilly's important so we'll find time. Are you alright with that?"

"I don't know what it is," she said.

She found out in about an hour, after she and her mum

had sipped sweet tea and talked through the episode a dozen times. Not once did Dilly mention the WiFi that shouldn't have been there or the story that had unfolded after, the story that she could tell no one, the one that happened in the blink of an eye and lasted, well, who was to say.

She feared the machine, a coffin-like metal tomb in which she lay. They'd given her an alert button to press in case she panicked. She wouldn't panic, she knew that. She wasn't the type. She was more the fainting type, she joked to herself. Would they scan her thoughts, her secrets, her memories? Would they see what they didn't want her to see? What was the point of this giant machine that all but gobbled her up. As it whirred into action, she breathed deeply, closed her eyes and thought of Simon.

0000 0100: SIMON

He cowered in the corner, afraid they would find him, telling himself not to be afraid but afraid nevertheless. He wanted his mum and dad to protect him, to shield him from all this... nastiness. It wasn't right. They'd never taught him what to do about such situations. They'd taught him how to work hard, how to do well at school, how to take pride in his appearance, how to respect his elders, how to be good, basically. They hadn't taught him how to deal with bullies. And nothing inside him revealed any secret answers. He was on his own.

They'd followed him from the main road where they'd asked for money. He had none to give but would have given them anything if it would have kept them away. That's the kind of boy he told himself he was, a coward. He hated himself for not having an answer. He didn't hate the bullies because they might feel his hate and hurt him even more. The dark was his friend. Here in the grey block, the shadowy basement where the caretaker stored brushes and pans and brooms and bottles of smelly bleach. They surely wouldn't find him here. There were eight blocks, almost identical, and others besides. They might search one or two or even three, but they couldn't search all of them. That was impossible. They might not search any at all. They would go home to their unloving, uncaring families and pretend everything was alright, when it wasn't. Just like he would. They might hunt him down relentlessly, like a wild beast. They might. They did not obey rules, these lawless boys.

He shook there in the corner, wondering if he would ever get out. He would have to at some point. Maybe he could live down there, pretend this was his home and stay there, safe and sound, away from all trouble. That was impossible. He would have to leave at some point, have to brave the outside world. Would they be there, waiting beyond the heavy wooden doors, standing like sentinels of doom with their fists ready to strike and their boots ready to kick?

In his imagination they took on nightmarish form. They were boys who would never eat, never sleep, who would spend their lives harrying him, poor little Simon, to death. They would never leave him alone. Whenever they found him, they would target him, because they knew he would be afraid, knew that he would never fight back. He tried to breathe deeply and think clearly.

Which was when he saw the ghost.

He blinked to make sure because the shadows in the darkness played tricks. He might be twelve years old but he wasn't stupid. He just had a 'riotous' imagination as his English teacher had told him. And it was rioting now. Like crazy. It was all Simon could do to keep still and keep breathing. The ghost shimmered and trembled, hunkered down in the corner, trying to pull itself up from the ground. Simon shook his head in disbelief, blinked again and said a quiet prayer to himself. 'Please don't let me die here all alone.' He didn't think about who the prayer was to, it was for Jesus. Mum and dad always told him that prayer was the answer to everything. That was about all they told him, apart from some proverbs, and generally he didn't pay much attention, but at this moment he did it automatically. Stay here and face this or dash out and face them. The devil and the deep blue sea.

The ghost shifted on to all fours.

Was it an animal after all, not a ghost? No, he could see through it, as if it were made of liquid glass. Simon backed away and the ghost turned a head full of curls and stared with two, faint, green eyes which opened wide when they saw him, or seemed to see him.

Simon didn't hesitate but acted purely on instinct. He dashed towards the doors, pushed them open and rushed out, fully expecting to be faced with Norman and his gang, smirking at their prey.

Nothing.

The area between the tomblike grey buildings was empty.

Simon headed straight for the playground where children were messing about on the swings, roundabout and seesaw. None of them paid him any attention and none of them were the ones he feared. He turned to look back. The ghost had not emerged from the basement. Or if it had, Simon couldn't see it in the cold light of day.

He hated himself at that moment. 'Run home to mummy' a voice cried in his head. 'Run home like the baby you are.' It was unfair. He felt that the world was pressing in on him. Who wouldn't be afraid? Thuggish big boys on one side and a ghost, for heaven's sake, on the other. He was shivering with fear and told himself for the umpteenth time to calm down. He really did try. He headed over to the railings near the canal and stood there, working to make sense of it all.

Someone waved to him and called his name. One of their neighbours, the mother of a school classmate.

"Are you alright, love?" He nodded. "Tell your mum I'll pop round to return the sugar. I managed to buy some. You sure you're alright. You look like you've seen a ghost."

"I have," whispered Simon.

She laughed and walked on.

Simon thought it strange how little others could see of him. His whole world was closing in and this wise adult hadn't a clue. She used an expression like his mum would have used but she didn't mean it. She didn't believe it.

Simon didn't want to go home. His mum would only

say the same things, things which he wanted to believe but found hard to accept, for some reason. They didn't quite gel with his own experiences of being endlessly bullied and having no answer to other boys' strength and aggression. He had none of these things in his heart so he didn't understand how others did. Now, he suspected, God had sent a ghost to torment him. Why else had it found him out, hiding away like that? Why couldn't it appear somewhere else, to someone else some other time? Because it was after him, that had to be answer. It had been sent to 'get' him. No one else, just him. If he told his mum and dad, they wouldn't believe a word of it. Why should they? They would tell him that Jesus had the answer and He was the one to listen to. If he listened to other voices, they were the voices of the devil.

The thing in the cellar haunted him already, just like ghosts were supposed to do. And yet, for all his fear, there was something about it which didn't look quite like the devil or a bad spirit were supposed to look. It wasn't green or red and smoky with horns and foul breath and hot and fiery, howling and crying to wake the dead. No, it was almost in pain itself, he thought, trying to raise itself, as if it was hurt.

Was he going to be afraid all his life? He wished he could be different. Well, just this once he would be. If anything bad happened to him, it wouldn't be for wanting to make something good happen instead. Besides, there was no real choice. There was no one to turn to.

He slowly made his way back to the basement of the grey block, the bullies almost out of his mind, thankfully. Even they took second place to a ghost. When he arrived, he tippy-toed back inside, hoping and believing that it had gone, even that it had never been there at all.

It took a few moments to accustom to the darkness. He squinted until his eyes focused again, then edged in deeper.

There it was, in the corner, transparent as a morning mist, quivering, but not with wicked intent, it seemed, but with fear. The ghost was sobbing.

As Simon approached, it looked up. A girl, definitely, with curly hair and green eyes, a green that shone through the milky whiteness of the spectral body.

"Who are you?"

The words met in mid-air and echoed around, for they both had asked the same question at the same moment, but the ghost's voice was distant, almost an echo itself.

"You first," said Simon.

"Why me?"

"Well, you're the ghost, aren't you?"

"The what?"

Simon repeated the word.

"Where am I?" the ghost asked.

"Don't you know?" Simon replied.

The ghost shook its head. It seemed terribly lost and afraid.

"I was in school. My first day. I took out my mobile. I saw the WiFi. I clicked it… and here I am."

Simon had no idea what the ghost was saying. She used words that had no meaning to him. He said so but it could not explain.

"I'm Simon," he said, as if that would solve all the puzzles in the world.

"Dilly," said the ghost.

They looked at each other, trying to figure out their intentions, fearing the worst but slowly realizing that they meant each other no harm.

"Why have you come back from the dead?" Simon asked.

Dilly's eyes opened wider than ever. Simon saw through them onto the brick wall behind. He feared they might grow so large that he would fall into them.

"I'm not dead," said Dilly. "At least, I don't think I am. You're the one that looks like a ghost."

Simon checked his hands and arms and body. He seemed as solid as ever.

"Prove it," he said. The Dilly ghost asked how. "What's behind me?" Simon asked.

The Dilly ghost glanced over and said, without hesitation, "A bucket, a mop, a cardboard box, a…"

"You're cheating," said Simon. "You knew what was there anyway. You saw it before I came back."

"I can still see them," said Dilly. "What do you mean, 'back'? I never saw you before."

"But I was here. I saw you arrive all crumpled up on the ground."

"Whatever you think, I can see through you."

"And I can see through you."

They each surveyed the other, cautiously, suspiciously, but there truly was no threat, just mystery.

"Perhaps we're both dead," said Dilly. "We died at the same time and this is heaven."

"Does it look like heaven?" asked Simon. "It's the caretaker's basement room. One of them. He has stores in every block. He'll be back soon. You'd better be gone before or he'll catch you."

Dilly could take none of this in. Basements and caretakers and grey blocks. Where on Earth was she? If it was heaven, then heaven was a shabby place, all bricks and stone and brushes and mops. Not an angel in sight.

"Then it's a dream," said Dilly. "That's what it is."

"Yours or mine?" Simon asked. "I mean, it could be either, except I wasn't asleep. I was… well, I was awake."

Dilly caught the hesitation and asked what he was doing. She needed to know exactly, to see whose dream this was, but Simon couldn't tell her. He couldn't say that he was running away from bullies. That would be embarrassing, especially to a girl. He shook his head and made up some story about playing with friends.

"I don't believe you," said Dilly. "You were asleep, you know it, and this is your dream."

"I wasn't. You're the one that fainted. You said so."

Dilly didn't know if she'd fainted or not, but certainly, the last thing she remembered was being somewhere totally different without a half invisible boy in funny clothes asking her peculiar questions. What *was* going on?

"I only said that I thought I fainted. When I touched..."

"There's no point telling me again," said Simon. "I don't understand half the words you said. But you're the one who isn't where they should be. I'm here, where I started. I haven't gone anywhere."

Dilly couldn't argue with that. She was certainly somewhere different and had to believe that Simon was telling the truth, that she had appeared to him, not the other way around. If this was not heaven, but was her dream, then why? She should dream about beautiful things, like trees and flowers, not a drab, claustrophobic room in a 'grey block', whatever that was. It was a grim imagining which she wanted to vanish, immediately. She shook her head, blinked three times, opened her eyes wide and stared.

"What are you doing?" Simon asked, thinking that Dilly might be a witch about to cast a spell on him.

"Trying to make you go away," she answered. "And this. All of it."

"It's my home," said Simon, softly. "Not this room, I mean. Outside. I can tell you what's out there because I live there. That would prove I'm telling the truth, wouldn't it? You couldn't, could you?" She couldn't. "Shall I?" he asked her?

"Shall you what?" Dilly asked.

"Describe what's outside, then you can come and see, and if I'm right, you'll know I'm telling the truth, that I'm real and you're not."

"Doesn't matter what you say," said Dilly, "I know I'm real. But go on, tell me anyway."

Dilly had in mind her new school grounds rather than her home as she was last there and saw no reason to think that she was anywhere else, apart from this dark nothingness of a basement. If she was dreaming, then she could be in Narnia or Middle Earth or Neverland, it didn't matter. If Simon was dreaming, then that didn't matter either because he would wake and all this would pop back into nothingness. What mattered was if Simon could describe exactly what was out there. She could prove it or disprove it by popping her head out of the door and looking around. She was bound to see the school, she felt sure of it because fainting didn't transport you anywhere, except onto the floor.

"There are eight grey blocks," said Simon, four pairs of two, each with eight floors, five flats to a floor."

"That's very exact," said Dilly.

Simon continued.

"On one side is a road and on the other a grassy play area running along the canal and the reservoir."

"There's a reservoir where I live," Dilly interrupted. "At least it used to be. It's a boating lake now."

"You can't boat on this," said Simon. "We drink the water. You can walk along the grassy bank to a playground with a swings, a roundabout, a see-saw…"

"A what?" Dilly asked.

"A see-saw. One of you goes up, the other goes down."

That made no sense to Dilly, but not much of this did, so she listened on.

"Around the playground there are more houses…"

"More grey blocks?"

"Brown blocks," said Simon. "Nicer. With four floors, not eight. There's a big green area with a tree in the middle.

You can see the playground from all the balconies, and the reservoir. We live on the top floor so you can see all of London some days.. There's a home for old people near where I live and a bus station at the end of the road. It's where some of the trolley buses stop."

Dilly looked blank.

"Buses with wires at the top?" Simon explained.

"Trams," said Dilly, and this time Simon looked blank.

"I think that's it," said Simon. "That's the best I can do. Now, if we go outside and you see all this, will you believe me, that I'm real and you're here."

Could she agree to it? If she did, what was she to make of it? To faint for no reason and find yourself in a totally different place. That was simply not possible. It had to be something going on in her head, but the only way to find the truth was to go along with it, for now. She had no choice.

"I don't promise anything," she said, "but I will go outside with you. Only…"

"Only what?"

"If people see you half invisible, what will I say?"

Simon laughed.

"It won't be me they see half invisible, it will be you! So what will I say?" he asked, emphasising the 'I'. "Come on," he said, "pop your head around the corner. Just look."

She followed him to the open double doorway. It was cloudy but bright, and beyond the doorway she could see nothing that she recognised but almost everything that Simon had described.

"I told you I was telling the truth," he said.

"So was I," whispered Dilly.

"Come out further," said Simon, "there's no one around."

He'd checked, of course, for the fear of seeing the big boys hanging around had not subsided. It lay there, like a wolf about to pounce. Dilly sensed his trepidation.

"You're nervous, too," she said, "of something."

Simon did not want to say anything about the bullies and his fears, but he was impressed how the Dilly ghost saw through him, in a different way to how he saw through her. Except... he stared.

"What's the matter?" she asked.

"You've gone!" he said.

"No, I'm here," said Dilly.

"I can't see you." Dilly had vanished into the bright daylight, like an optical illusion. "Come back inside."

Dilly stepped into the shadowy area and became half visible again.

"Well?" she asked.

"I see you," whispered Simon, smiling, even though it was a puzzle beyond solving. "How strange!" Dilly walked back out again and vanished. "Gone," said Simon.

Dilly walked further out, studying the landscape of buildings. It was just as Simon had painted it for her. There were the grey blocks, truly grey concrete, with curtained windows, long balconies, doors painted a slightly darker grey. She could see a long grassy verge and perhaps the twinkle of water beyond. In the other direction, buses could be seen clunking along a road, attached by poles to wires hanging overhead, just as Simon had told her.

And it was all as solid as you like.

In the daylight, Simon and his world shifted into focus. Dilly saw it as if it were real, which it surely had to be, despite the mystery of it being there. It seemed that as daylight made her fade from Simon, it made him more real to her. What was going on? Was she on another planet? Had she fallen through some Dr Who type hole in space into this... this alien world? Simon did not seem like an alien and all these peculiar buildings seemed wholly Earthly. She reached out to touch the wall of the building and her hand went straight through the concrete. She stared, and Simon laughed.

"It's not funny," she said.

"No, I know, but it's interesting, don't you think? I love science. It's my favourite subject at school. I want to know how and why things happen, and my science teacher says that there are reasons for everything, so there has to be a reason for this. Doesn't there?"

Dilly withdrew her hand and shook her head.

"It isn't possible," she whispered.

"Lots of things seem impossible. Think of television. All those black and white pictures every evening. They are impossible but they happen. We watched the coronation last week and it was like we were all there. You should have seen it!"

Dilly was staring at Simon as if he were talking gibberish. He was squinting at where she ought to be, looking through a hazy cloud of eyelashes, trying to make her out.

"Black and white? Coronation? What coronation?"

"Princess Elizabeth, silly. What coronation do you think? I can see you, just," he said, squinting harder than ever.

"On a black and white television?"

Simon sensed Dilly's confusion and explained, as if she were from Mars.

"It's a kind of a wooden box with a glass screen. Cameras can film something far away and make it appear inside the box, behind the glass. Mum and dad bought one just for the coronation. Lots of people did. Actually, I think almost everyone did. I'd like to find out how it works, though. You'll be amazed if you see it."

Dilly was staring open mouthed, but not at the idea of a black and white wooden box that could show pictures of something happening miles away, but at the implication of what Simon was telling her.

"Are you still there?" he asked, looking around, "I lost you for a minute."

"I'm here."

"Ah, yes," he said, "If I squint, I can make you out. I bet you can't believe everything I've told you."

Dilly did not know what to say. There was too much going on in her head to spill out everything in one go. Besides, Simon was so suddenly excited that she didn't want to burst his bubble. He seemed like such a kind boy, and most unusual. He'd been worried about something, that was clear, but for a few moments the worry had vanished and he was telling her, of all things, about television.

"Mum and dad were riveted," he said, "you should have seen them. They never get excited, never, but they did for this. They invited my uncles and aunts to come, the ones who couldn't afford televisions, I mean, and we all gathered around and it was special. Just that once, it was special. I never like being at home that much, but I don't like being out either," he said, which was a sad thing to admit. "It was worth it though. Honestly, it was like magic. I wish I knew how they did it!"

Dilly had grown up with TV screens like cinemas, thin as a wafer, with countless ways to see a zillion programmes. If anyone couldn't believe anything, it would be Simon who wouldn't believe that. But she said nothing except, "It sounds wonderful," and he smiled into the air, hearing her tell his story of the coronation.

"I would have liked to have gone," he said. "Mum wanted to but dad said we should watch it on the new television. That's why we got it in the first place. That's why everyone got it. There's other stuff, but that was the real reason. And the next day, that's all we talked about. It was all we talked about. She was so pretty, the queen. I wish you'd seen it."

Dilly had seen it, only seventy five years later in 2022. As weird as it sounded, that was the only explanation. This dream was nothing if not true to itself.

"Hello?"

Simon had lost her again.

"I'm here," she said.

"I see you," he said, blinking and squinting like mad. "Don't you believe me, Dilly?"

"Every word, truly," she replied. Could she tell Simon what she believed. Maybe, but not yet. Best to wait and see what happened. She noticed for the first time how old fashioned Simon was dressed. It was so obvious now, she wondered how she'd missed it in the first place, but she had. He wore short, grey trousers held up by a brown belt, a grey shirt and grey socks with black shoes. He could have been a ghost himself, all greys, like that.

"I'm glad you've come here," said Simon. "I don't know why you're here but I'm glad."

"I don't know why either," said Dilly, "but there has to be a reason. My mum says there are reasons for everything."

"You've got a mum? Can ghosts could have mms?"

"You've got one, and you're still a ghost to me."

They were never going to convince each other, although Dilly had to admit, this was probably not her world, but if it was, then it was not her time. She was certain that she was not a ghost, and if Simon wasn't either, then what was he? A rather lost, frightened boy by the looks of him.

"I have," said Simon, "and a dad, and I need to go home now. They'll be worried. Well, mum will."

"You can't leave me," said Dilly, "not on my own, not here."

Here was a dilemma. Both were scared of certain things, in their own ways, but Dilly was the most in need. Simon saw that, despite his fear of the big boys appearing any moment and tormenting him yet again. Dilly was alone and lost and he could not leave her.

"Come back with me," he said. "Follow. No one can see you in the light if they don't squint."

She did, staring at every single thing on the way, realising how accurately Simon had described the neighbourhood. Nobody glanced at her but then nobody glanced at Simon either, except when he spoke to her and appeared to be talking to himself. They passed the blocks of flats, the playground, the road, the reservoir, it was all as Simon described, and all clean, proud and new. New! Houses were not built like this any more. She, of all people, knew that, living in her gleaming, giant greenhouse. And yet there was nothing old about any of it. It was fresh and clean and lovely. She couldn't understand why Simon seemed so shy about it. There was something troubling him for he kept scouting around anxiously. Yet to Dilly, there was nothing here that seemed threatening. She would happily give up her tower for this. There was space and simplicity and a community spirit. Whoever planned this had people in mind, not rabbits, and not money. She sensed that as clear as day. The grass, the playground, the water, the sidewalks, the trees, the planted balconies – there was room to breathe. Where was it, she wondered. More importantly, when was it?

"Here it is," said Simon. "This is where I live."

He looked relieved to be there, as if he'd just navigated a dangerous minefield rather than a delightful walk across a green and pleasant land.

Like Simon had said, he lived on the top floor of a house that, despite being a block of flats, still looked like a house of its own. The balcony stretched from one side to the other passing six front doors. Simon's was the last. They'd gone up the stairs despite there being a lift as Simon seemed reluctant to get in it.

"Isn't it safe?" Dilly asked.

"It's safe," he replied, "but I like the stairs."

She didn't believe him. There were four floors divided into two, so eight flights altogether and she was out of breath when they reached the top.

The view was wonderful. Where she and mum lived was equally wonderful, maybe more so, but this was still impressive.

"You can see St. Paul's," said Simon. "Look."

He pointed out the distant dome and Dilly at once realised that this was indeed London. Not the London she saw from her home, but London nevertheless. There was just as much building work going on, maybe more, with swathes of flattened land close by.

"It's from the war," said Simon. "This place was flat as a pancake, dad says. They've only just finished rebuilding it. Moment of truth," he said.

Dilly understood. Simon knocked on the door as he didn't have a key of his own. A woman answered, almost the spitting image of Simon, but older and rather careworn.

"Hello, darling. Late as usual. Come on. Tea's ready."

Simon's mother had eyes only for her son, but as Dilly crept in, she jumped as if startled and exclaimed, 'Oooh!'

Simon said nothing.

His home was neat and tidy with stuff that might have been more suited to a museum or vintage shop. If this was a dream, Dilly thought, it was still a most accurate and realistic one. Every detail was true to itself, true to this depiction of a past time. But was it a depiction? It was to Dilly as real as her own world, only she was not real to it - Simon's parents had absolutely no sense of there being a stranger in their home.

They shared the preparation of tea. His father, quiet and serious, helped out, each knowing what to do and when to do it. A copper kettle whistled, a clothes mangle was pushed into one corner, a heavy saucepan spat steam up onto a clothes airer fixed across the ceiling, a massive gas oven hissed and tins decorated with pictures of the young queen sat on a simple wooden table.

"How was school today?" his mother asked.

"Fine," Simon replied.

"Just fine?"

Simon was uncomfortable, hiding two secrets – the bullying and the ghost. He wondered if he would ever have to hide such secrets again. He excused himself and hurried into his bedroom.. He didn't need to beckon the Dilly ghost – it was right behind him.

"Stay here," he whispered. "You don't want to watch us eat, do you? I won't be long."

Dilly would have been an uncomfortable invisible intruder and told Simon to go. Strangely, she felt no pangs of hunger herself. Wherever she was and whatever had brought her here, as a ghost or vision, she was in food limbo.

Dilly stood ill at ease in Simon's bedroom, feeling desperately alone. She looked around, partly out of curiosity, partly to keep out the heeby jeebies. There were books on shelves and books on the bed and books on the floor. Clearly, Simon read profusely. All of them had hard covers and colourful covers, comic annuals as well as encyclopaedias, puzzle books, histories and science. There were toys, too, a white garage with dinky toy cars and a castle with tin soldiers standing to attention. There were no posters and no computers, laptops, mobiles, televisions or other technology. Again, it was like a room from a museum. To liven it up, there was a small fish tank with a couple of goldfish enjoying life.

She heard the family talking, even though she felt impolite listening. They were in the next room and the sound carried. Despite knowing Simon for barely thirty minutes, she liked him and felt rather sorry for him. His mother clucked around like the proverbial hen whilst his father seemed to be in a world of his own and said little. Simon's mother questioned him about school, worried him about his health and fretted over every possible wrong turn he might make in life.

"I'll be alright mum," he said, over and over it seemed to Dilly.

Dilly pushed her face against the wall and found herself slipping through the brick, peering into the dining room. Not even Simon noticed, but if he had, he might have choked on his food, but it gave Dilly some comfort to be with people, even like this.

Simon's mother kept questioning him and his father kept eating. He seemed like a kind man, affected by whatever he had seen in battlefields across the world, but when Simon got slightly peeved with a question his mother had asked and raised his voice, his father tapped the table and said, "Don't you raise your voice to your mother, Simon, don't you dare," quietly but with authority. Simon looked contrite and even Dilly realised that there was more going on than she could see. The meal may have been a regular family occasion but there was a lot bubbling away beneath the surface.

"Are you sure you're alright?" Simon's mother asked for the umpteenth time. "You look uncomfortable, Simon."

"No, I'm fine," he replied. "Can I leave the table and go out now? We won't be long. I mean, I won't be long."

Dilly was surprised to see that his parents let him out by himself. It was evening, almost dusk. There was no way any parent she knew would let their children roam free at that time, at least not as far as Dilly believed. But they didn't blink an eyelid and he went back into his bedroom, squinted to find the Dilly ghost and hurried her out side.

"I watched," Dilly admitted. "Couldn't help it. Put my

head through the wall like a proper ghost. Your mum's a bit of a worrier isn't she?"

"I'm her only son. I wish I had a brother or a sister, but I don't."

"And your dad, he doesn't ever hit you, does he, Simon?"

"No! Why would you say that?"

"The way he tapped the table, it felt like a warning."

"He wouldn't hit me. He loves me," said Simon. Like most children, their parents had been caught up in the war. Simon himself had been born right in the middle of it when no one knew what was going to happen. "He was a soldier," he said "He fought all over the world. He's brave. He wouldn't hit me, and if he did, I'd probably have deserved it. They both love me, they have different ways of showing it. Did you really put your head through the wall?"

"I was lonely in your room. Sorry. I didn't mean to be nosey." Dilly didn't want to upset Simon who looked troubled enough already. "You look pale," she said, changing the subject.

"So do you. I should have saved you some food. Aren't you hungry?"

Dilly told him that for whatever reason, she wasn't hungry at all.

"Ghosts don't need to eat," she said, "apparently."

"Ah," exclaimed Simon, "you admit it!"

"I don't admit anything. I don't know what's going on but obviously it's not normal, is it. I don't usually become invisible and end up in the past like Dr Who."

"The past? What do you mean? Like which doctor?"

Dilly hadn't meant to tell Simon what she believed, but she had to, now.

"I don't know for sure," she said, "but everything you've said and everything I've seen, it's like things were in history."

"In history? Like William the Conqueror?"

"Not like him, no, that was real history. Like you said, the coronation."

"So?"

"What year was that?"

"This year, silly, two weeks ago."

"See? For me, it wasn't two weeks ago. It was seventy years ago."

Simon laughed.

"You are silly," he said.

"What year is is it now?" Dilly asked.

When Simon said '1952', Dilly whispered, "I knew it."

"Knew what?"

She explained as best she could what she thought was happening, and although Simon found it hard to believe, the fact was, a half invisible girl was standing there talking to him. He loved science and he knew that wonderful things were being discovered all the time, but this might be a wonder too far.

They made their way back to the basement store room, not for any particular reason except it was where Dilly had appeared and maybe the place where she could get back to wherever she belonged. They stopped by the fence near the reservoir, Simon talking to thin air again.

"It's quite difficult to believe, Dilly."

He spoke so earnestly and ardently, almost like an adult, it touched her.

"It's just as hard for me to believe I'm here," she replied.

"Not totally here," he said.

"Not totally, no."

"So what were you doing before.. before you popped up here?" Simon asked.

"I was at school," Dilly replied, and then realised that there were a hundred words she'd have to use which Simon wouldn't understand. How could she tell him about mobile phones and 5G and all that stuff when he was in raptures about a wooden television? "Maybe I just fainted after all," she said. "It's easier to believe than this."

"Except that I'm real," said Simon.

"Except that," said Dilly, "but you only believe you're real."

"I don't only believe it," said Simon. "I've been real for twelve years, almost thirteen."

"I've been real for thirteen, almost fourteen," said Dilly.

It was certainly a puzzle, one that they couldn't unravel easily, and it became even more peculiar when Dilly said, "It was my first day, too."

"First day where?"

"At school. We'd only moved in a few weeks ago, during the holidays, so this was my first day. I mean it *is* my first day. I will be back, I know I will."

"It's a new school for me, too," said Simon. "We moved a few months ago so I'm new, too. We're both new, aren't we?"

Dilly tried to make sense of the puzzle. Something had happened to bring her back to this time and to this place. But what was it? And what was 'this place'? She stared at the houses all around her, old and new at the same time. She turned towards the narrow road connecting the estate to the more distant main road and then to the grass verge of the canal, running as far as she could see in every direction. Beyond it was the reservoir that served Simon's home and a thousand other homes with fresh water. It was similar in shape to the boating lake near her new home. Very similar. A little revelation opened up in front of her.

"Simon, suppose... suppose this is where I live!" He didn't understand what she meant. "The reservoir, it's the same shape as the boating lake. And the road, the canal, this green verge, they're not that different."

"So?"

"Well, maybe this is where I live, only then, not now, 'now' for me, I mean."

"But you don't recognise any of it. You said so."

"Seventy years, it's a very long time. Things get old and fall down, don't they?"

"But this is new," said Simon. "They've only just finished it. They started soon after the war ended in 1945. We only moved in last year. It should last forever."

"Nothing lasts forever," said Dilly. "I can't prove it, but I bet I'm right."

There was nothing of her home here, nothing at all except distorted reflections. The rest of Simon's home might have been on Mars, and perhaps it was, if this was a dream, yet she felt that she was right, that this had all been demolished for flashy, modern glass homes, including hers.

"Where's your school?" she asked Simon.

He pointed and said, "I walk it. About fifteen minutes. That way."

"Mine's further away," said Dilly, "but that doesn't mean anything. They're always closing schools and opening new ones. This is very peculiar, Simon."

"I agree with that," he said.

"Tell me something," Dilly asked, inquisitively, "what were you hiding from? What *are* you hiding from?"

A little boy in a gloomy basement all by himself wasn't normal, not in her time and not in this time, either. Simon shrugged and said he was doing nothing, just thinking.

"I like to think," he said. "I think about what I'm going to do when I'm grown up and clever. I want to invent things and make the world a better place."

"So you hid under a great big block of flats... to think?"

He shrugged again.

"Well, I don't believe you," said Dilly, "and I don't see why you can't tell me the truth."

"I haven't told any lies," said Simon.

"No, but you haven't told me the truth, and that's a kind of lie."

Simon looked extremely uncomfortable. He pulled away and walked on, looking around in the way he had soon after the Dilly ghost had appeared.

"That's all I'm going to say. It's not important. What matters now is you."

Even Dilly had to admit that this was true. Here she was, stuck in a place she did not belong, in a time she did not belong, with no obvious way to get home.

"E.T. call home," she said. Simon looked mystified. "Doesn't matter. Let's head back to where you found me. Maybe you can say what you were doing there in the first place. It might be a clue, you never know."

The reservoir sparkled beyond the long grass verge and the fence. Dusk was falling and Dilly was still impressed that Simon could stay out like this. Other people were out too, adults and children, walking, playing, apparently without a worry in the world. Dilly waited for Simon to spill the beans about what he was doing lurking around all by himself in a dark, dank store room but he was reluctant to talk.

"Were you meeting your girlfriend there?" Dilly joked.

Simon just blushed and whispered, "No, course not."

If he'd been skulking around a library, she could have understood that. She couldn't understand him skulking in that place, though. Unless…. She had an idea.

"Were you hiding?"

"Why would I hide?" he replied, a bit too quickly.

"Oh, many reasons. Were you bunking off school?"

"Bunking?"

"Missing."

"No, I like school."

"Well, it's not normal."

She looked askance at him and followed her intuition.

"Simon?" she asked. He blinked, afraid of what she was going to ask. "Are you being bullied?"

The question hit home. Simon stopped still, blushed even more, in a different way, and said.

"You mustn't say, not to anyone."

"I'm hardly likely to, am I?" Dilly said, "No one can see me or hear me except you. It's true, then, someone's after you?" He looked away, not wanting to catch her eye. "That's horrible," said Dilly, "but you must tell someone. How about Child Line?" Simon didn't know what that was. "What about your teachers? Your mum and dad?"

"It would only make things worse," said Simon, "especially mum and dad. She would be worried sick all day every day and he wouldn't know what to do. The war turned him upside down and inside out. That's what mum says. I mean, she loves him, but he doesn't like to get involved in anything. All he wants is a peaceful life, mum says."

"But you're their son. They have to do something. Who's doing it?"

"I don't want to talk about it," Simon insisted. "It will go away."

Dilly hated bullies. When she was eight, an older girl had targeted her. It hadn't developed, luckily, but she knew the effect it could have on others. She had a fine sense of right and wrong, born with it, her mum said, and injustices upset her terribly. The world seemed so full of them, too. On the news, in the things people said and did, in the things she heard, in the things she felt, there were countless wrongs. It was impossible to stamp them all out. They were like weeds. You stamped on one and another grew next to it. You cut one away but there were always more. And bullying was the worst. If you didn't stop it in the bud, it would blossom into who knew what – people oppressing people, groups oppressed groups, nations killing nations, and she saw that what was happening to Simon was dangerous. She wished she could see the boy or boys who were doing this to him.` She'd give him what for. A gang, probably, maybe one lousy ringleader. Not maybe, definitely.

How was this so definite? Because there they were, loitering like criminals near the entrance to the basement.

For a moment, Dilly thought they'd done what she'd done, appearing out of nowhere, but no, they'd been wandering aimlessly and bumped into Simon as he approached the grey block. What happened next took Dilly by surprise because it happened so quickly. The biggest boy pushed Simon in the chest so hard that he stumbled backwards and fell over. The other boys laughed. There were five of them altogether, but the leader was clearly the tall, large set older boy with red hair, a noticeable gap in his front teeth and cruel eyes. Dilly despised him the moment she saw him. He might have hit her too, had he seen her, but she was invisible to all of them. They pushed Simon around, and when he fell, one of them trod on his hand, another on his leg. Dilly watched in horror. Simon didn't cry, but he didn't fight back, either. He tried to get up and they pushed him over again. One of them ransacked Simon's pockets and took his money. Not much, but even a farthing would have been a crime. The big boy grabbed Simon by the collar and eyeballed him, threatening him if he opened his mouth to anyone.

Dilly could not bear it, could not watch such violence and remain quiet.

"Leave him, leave him, leave him!" she screamed, her sense of injustice strong within her.

The sequence of events then was rapid. Simon sat up, fighting back tears. Four of the boys stood like statues whilst the red headed leader took a step back, raising his fist, staring madly at the spot the words came from.

"What the hell?" he whispered.

"Dilly, run away!" Simon shouted. "Run. I'll be alright. Just run away!"

The words echoed in her head. Her own words, she was sure of it, but that was all she was sure of, because everything faded – the gang, the houses, the basement, and Simon, too.

"No!" she cried out. "Not now! Simon! Simon!"

But it was no good. Whatever force had brought her there was taking her back. Within seconds, she was in the school playground surrounded by countless astonished eyes and a teacher leaning over her, asking if she was alright.

0000 0101: LAURA

"Good news," said the doctor to Dilly's mother after the MRI scan revealed its results. "There is nothing obvious to be seen but we'd like to keep her in one night, if you don't mind."

"I don't want to stay in," said Dilly. "I'm alright, really I am."

"You don't know that, darling," her mother said. "The doctors know best."

Dilly looked downcast, despite the news. She didn't feel ill at all and although she was still haunted by the intensity of all that had happened, she wasn't worried, at least not for herself. In fact, she was hopeful that it would happen again so that she could make sure Simon was okay. Normally, if she'd dreamed, she didn't want to revisit the dreamscape to end it properly, like a book she wanted to finish. Here, though, she was anxious. She truly believed Simon, somewhere, sometime, no matter how long ago, needed her help, and she was desperate to give it.

"I know I'm alright. If I wasn't, I'd tell you."

The doctor had a word with her colleague then agreed.

"Here is our number. If you're at all unwell during the night, or any time, phone and tell us. We will bring you in at once."

"I won't be unwell," said Dilly. "I promise."

"Sadly, no one can promise such things," said the doctor. "But I'm confident you will be okay. We'll make another appointment for next week, have a chat and see how you are."

"Can she go to school?" Dilly's mum asked.

Dilly didn't know whether she wanted the doctor to say

yes or no. On one hand, she wanted to join in as quickly as possible, on the other, she could imagine the inevitable chatter for 'the girl who fainted'.

"I'll leave that up to you," said the doctor. "If Dilly feels up to it, then fine, if not, then rest at home."

The rest of the day was punctuated with calls from various people including Miss Roberts, anxious to know how things had gone. Dilly just said 'fine'. It was impossible to explain the MRI to anyone. She'd been stuck inside the giant machine for what seemed like an eternity, during which time all she could think of was rescuing Simon. Luckily, the scan could not put her imagination or memories on any computer screen so nobody had a clue as to what was going on inside her head, not her real, invisible head, only the visible one.

That was until about seven o'clock in the evening when there was a knock on the door and there stood little Laura, face as anxious as it had been in the morning.

"Yes?" said Dilly's mother.

"I'm Dilly's friend, Laura," she said, softly.

"Really?" said Dilly's mother. "She's only been at school five minutes. She wasn't well."

"I know," said Laura, "I was there. I've been thinking about her all day. The secretary gave me your address. He said you wouldn't mind."

"She's tired and sleeping," fibbed Dilly's mother, a little peeved that their address should be given out so freely, but Laura seemed like a quiet and sensible girl, and Dilly needed a new friend now more than ever.

"I'm not sleeping now, mum," said Dilly, popping her head around her mother's back to see who was there. "Hello Laura."

"You remember me!"

"Course I do. It was only a few hours ago."

"I thought you'd forget."

Dilly's mother was outnumbered and agreed to let Laura in, 'but not for long'.

Dilly told her new friend all about the MRI and that they'd found nothing wrong.

"People faint all the time," said Laura, as if every pupil in the school dropped to the ground regularly. "It's normally something to do with blood flowing from the head too quickly."

Impressed, Dilly said, "I wasn't doing anything though, just standing there using my phone."

They sat on cushions on the floor and swapped life stories. Laura said that she was the middle of three children with a brother and a sister on either side. They hadn't been where they were for long, same as Dilly. They were both 'new'. But Laura did not say where her family had come from, only that her parents' work shifted them around a lot. She felt sorry for Dilly being the only one, and even more sorry when she heard that Dilly had no father, at least not one on site to do fatherly things.

"Things happen for a reason," said Dilly, sagely, "although I would have liked him to stick around for another twenty years or so."

Laura laughed, a gentle, honest chuckle. Then she asked Dilly the one question Dilly really didn't know how to answer. "Who is Simon?" said Laura. "You were going on about him when you woke up."

Dilly had an important decision to make. Either she lied to Laura or told the unbelievable truth. If she lied, Laura might know. For one thing, Dilly was a terrible liar. She couldn't do it to save the planet. And even if she could, she would have to live with the lie forever and it would sour her new friendship. If she told the truth, however, Laura might still not believe her. She hardly believed it herself. There was no proof and it might well have been an illusion. The MRI could see a lot, but it couldn't see her imagination or her dreams.

"If I tell you, you'll think I'm lying, or mad or something."

"You're not mad, Dilly."

This time, Dilly laughed. Laura was the most open and straightforward person.

"But something peculiar happened."

Laura waited and so did Dilly, then began recounting exactly what had happened, every detail, bringing the whole strange experience back to life. Laura listened without interrupting and without giving away anything of what she was thinking. When Dilly had finished, Laura said quietly.

"All in a moment? That's as long as you were out for."

"All in about a moment. Yes."

"I believe you," said Laura. Dilly's eyes opened wide. Such trust. "Time is like the Tardis," Laura added, "bigger on the inside than the outside. And it started when you held your phone?"

"And connected to a WiFi that shouldn't have been there."

"Can I see?" Laura asked.

Dilly showed the phone and listed all the WiFi connections. The YpHi one was not there.

"It was there this morning," said Dilly. "And at the supermarket. It comes and goes, but not in the same places."

"Who set up your new home?" Laura asked.

"Mum called them. I forget." Dilly said.

"You could find out and ask them, but I don't think they'd help. It's quite strange, Dilly."

"True," said Dilly, "What could I ask them? Not everyone's as nice as you. Besides, it won't be easy. Mum had to wait weeks before they came. And it's all done automatically, you know, 'Press 1 to do this, Press 2 to do that.' I don't think mum spoke to anyone at all, just robot voices. It's a strange name," Dilly said, "I mean the WiFi one. Do you think it means something?"

"WiFi names don't mean anything, usually," Laura replied, "What could it mean?"

They had no idea. Like Laura said, they were simply letters and numbers, as obscure as the user could make them. They used Dilly's tablet to search for it on the wonderful internet which often had answers to everything, but not to this.

"Your Profile Has Incinerated," said Laura.

"Sorry?"

"You Prefer Hot Ice cream."

Dilly looked at Laura as if she was the one making up stories, but she was only making up possible acronyms for the missing connection.

"Yesterdays Problems Have... erm... Invisibilised."

Dilly caught on.

"Yaks Prefer Hungry Insects."

"Good one," said Laura. "Well, I won't forget it now. What a mystery."

"There were numbers after it, too," said Dilly. "Lots."

"You're supposed to have names you can remember. Was there anything special about them?"

Dilly tried to remember but hadn't a clue. They looked like random numbers then and she could not remember them now.

"It's great of you to believe me," she said. "It's a bit weird, isn't it."

"Totally weird," said Laura, "but that makes it interesting. What else can we try?"

There was one thing that Dilly had left out of her story, perhaps the most important thing.

"I did have one idea," she admitted, "though it might sound far out."

"It's all far out," said Laura. "Tell me."

So Dilly explained her idea that the place she'd seen was the very place they were in now, only seventy years ago, before the people building these glass monstrosities were born.

"What made you think that?" Laura asked.

"The lake, mainly," Dilly replied. "It was the same shape as the reservoir there. And the grass verge, and some of the paths between the houses. It's hard to explain, I just felt it."

"Female intuition," said Laura, wisely. "We could investigate," she added.

Dilly had thought of this. The internet was a wonderful encyclopaedia of everything, and a bit more, too. She'd thought of seeing what her new home had once looked like but was afraid of what she might see. She half hoped that whatever had happened to her had been an illusion, and if she looked and found nothing, then an illusion it would have been. But if she found an exact replica, then it surely had to have been real, there was no other explanation.

"You have to know," said Laura. "Better we find out than keep guessing."

If it was not true, then Dilly could forget Simon and the bullies and his odd parents, they would all be fiction – characters in a story. But if it was true, she would have to find a way to help him. How? She did not know, but she was a determined sort of girl.

They powered up Dilly's tablet but Dilly let Laura do the searching. She sat beside her friend and watched, fingers crossed, but crossed for what, she did not know.

There were a few pages of text about the current building, with pictures that made it look like some kind of comic book city. All it needed was Superman leaping between tall buildings.

"Why did you come here?" Laura asked.

"Mum wanted to. It's posh. She likes posh."

Laura laughed.

"We came because, well, it seemed like the right thing to do."

That was a peculiar answer, but Laura was a little mystery in herself, full of secrets, Dilly thought.

"Mum really wanted this. I'll get used to it, I suppose."

"You will," said Laura, wisely. She had something of the grown up about her, as if she knew more than her thirteen years ought to know.

Ploughing through pages of images on the web, they couldn't seem to get a definitive answer as to whether Dilly's trip was real or imagined. There were snippets of streets and buildings that Dilly thought might have been the ones she'd seen, but they could have been anywhere. Designs were similar in many parts of the country at that time, just as they were now.

They stopped after half an hour with no decision.

"Do you think it will happen again?" Dilly asked.

Laura hesitated in her seat as if wanting to say more but unsure whether or not to say it.

"If it does, there will be a reason," she said, finally. "There normally is, for most things."

Dilly once again saw that glint of mystery in Laura's eyes, hard for her to pin down, but definitely there. Nevertheless, they were the kindest of eyes and Dilly was glad that Laura had befriended her. She was grateful too that Laura trusted her completely. Even amongst the friends she'd left behind, even Abi, she could not think of anyone who would have accepted the impossible story so readily and been so keen to help. Perhaps she and mum had come here for the right reasons after all, and maybe Laura had come her way for the right reasons, too. Time would tell, even if it was bigger on the inside than the outside.

0000 0110: Miss Roberts

Dilly slept well that night, which was a surprise considering all that had happened. Her mother popped in and out to make sure she was okay and in the morning asked her about ten times if she was sure she wanted to go to school. Dilly was sure. She'd arranged for Laura to come and meet her just after eight and Laura was nothing if not punctual.

"Be sure to tell the teachers if you have a headache," said mum. "Anything at all, darling, don't be shy. If you feel faint or…"

"I'll be fine, mum. Please don't worry."

When they arrived at school, Dilly was a celebrity, the girl who'd fainted on her first day. One of the crueller minds tried to take the mickey but was sent to Coventry where she growled and fretted alone. Everyone else was kind and intrigued. Dilly wondered what Abi would say with all this fuss and attention. She hadn't received any such thing in her old life. Maybe she should faint once a day to keep it going, she thought, and smiled to herself, but no, she preferred not to be in the limelight.

Fortunately, the next few days passed without incident. The teachers were ultra delicate with her, especially Miss Roberts who turned out to be Dilly's Head of House and pastoral carer. That was why Dilly found herself in Miss Roberts's office a week later, making sure everything was alright.

"How are you settling in?" she asked.

"Fine, miss."

"No more moments?"

Dilly had noticed that both staff and pupils expected a repeat performance. It was strange how reputations stuck, like labels. It was hard to unpeel something like this. The pupils might remember it for years to come, only because it was something different.

"No miss."

"I hear that the hospital have spoken to your mother. They can't find anything wrong at all. It's a mystery."

Dilly was hardly going to tell her teacher about peculiar internet connections, there one second, gone the next. That would have pigeon holed her forever in a way she really did not want. She would have liked to forget the entire episode, but Simon's plight still worried her. She so wanted him to be well and happy and safe. Leaving him in that horrible situation made her uneasy. She dreaded a repeat show in front of the school, but she would have done even that to rescue him, or make sure he was well.

Her mind wandered for a moment so she missed some of what her teacher was saying, until something snapped her back to the here and now.

"It isn't easy, moving, is it?" Miss Roberts asked.

"No miss."

"My family moved many times, but strangely, my great grandparents were here, all those years ago. Or was it great great...? I get mixed up," she laughed. "I never knew them, but they were here, just after the war."

"Really, miss?" Dilly asked, suddenly fully there. "Yes, really. Are you interested in history, Dilly?"

"I am, miss, yes."

"So you know about the Second World War?"

"Bits. It's on telly a lot."

Miss Roberts laughed, but it was a laugh tinged with worry. Such serious world changing events slipped into insignificance so quickly. Even in her own life of twenty-eight years, she'd seen headline events disappear from memory. But the 'telly' kept things alive, sometimes too long, she thought, and not always in the right way.

"If only they'd had cameras at the Battle of Hastings or Waterloo, what do you think, Dilly?"

"Yes, miss. They were 1066 and 1816."

"1815, Dilly, but pretty good. My heart sings. Your last school must have taught you well."

"It was okay, miss."

"And you had friends there, of course?"

"Abi. But she's gone funny on me."

"How so?"

Dilly shrugged.

"Jealous?"

"A little."

"Ah," said Miss Roberts, "money comes between us in so many ways. Like love." This time Dilly laughed. "You'll see, one day," said her teacher.

Dilly wanted to get back to Miss Roberts' own history. If her family had lived here, she might know a little about what it used to be like, but she didn't know how to ask without sounding too curious. Luckily, Miss Roberts helped her along.

"What were we saying, Dilly? Oh yes, old schools, moving and so on. Yes, change is part of life. People seem to change homes and schools nowadays like they change clothes. They didn't use to. My family were here for a long time, then my grandfather moved away, his children moved even further away, and that included my father, but I came back. Full circle."

"Yes, miss. I don't suppose…"

"You don't suppose what, Dilly?"

"Your grandfather ever told you what it was like here?"

Miss Roberts thought for a moment then said, "A little. He liked it most of the time and did well here. He had friends and went to a good school. It was different. You can tell, can't you. Look at all the building going on. It will never stop, will it?"

"You came back, though, miss."

"I did. I'm a glutton for punishment."

"Are you, miss?"

Miss Roberts did well to stop herself laughing. She saw a lot of her own personality in this rather shy, clever girl.

"Not really, just an expression."

"I wonder…" Dilly began. Miss Roberts waited. "Do you think your grandfather might have any photos of it here, like it was then?"

"I don't know. I'll phone him and ask, if you like?"

"Is he still alive, miss? Gosh!"

"Yes, he is, in his eighties now. I talk to him every couple of weeks. I'll ask. It's lovely that you're interested. Is it a project that you're working on?"

"Kind of, miss. With Laura."

"Ah, the enigmatic Laura."

Dilly looked puzzled and said, "Is that good, miss?"

"It's neither good nor bad. It means mysterious."

"She's nice, miss."

"Extremely. Her family only moved here recently. You see, it's a world of movement. Wouldn't do to stand still."

"No, miss."

"You mustn't be unhappy here, Dilly. In fact, I know you won't be."

"But our home, miss, it's so… different."

"Ah, you are in one of the new tower blocks, aren't you? Yes. They are a bit forbidding. Very different from…?" Dilly told her where they'd come from. "… the seaside? Of course, I remember. My goodness, that *is* different. Still, there's a lot going on here, too. Have you joined any clubs yet?"

"Reading and Drama and Science."

"Marvellous," said Miss Roberts.

She was true to her word. In a few days she called both Dilly and Laura into her office. As teachers' offices go, it was artistic, with tasteful prints and artwork of one kind or another balancing out the paperwork and files. Miss Roberts was a dedicated teacher, but had she trod a different path, she would have liked to have been an artist, furnishing the best galleries with unmade beds, automobile parts and the like. Dilly had already told Laura that she'd spoken to their teacher so they were expecting a mountain of photographs, but no, not one.

"It was different then in many ways," said Miss Roberts. "Now you can take a zillion photos and see them immediately, but then, every one was special. It took skill to take a photo and weeks to see it."

"Weeks, miss?" Dilly asked.

"You had to finish a roll of film first, sometimes 36 pictures, then send it to developers, and yes, that took weeks. Grandpa remembered his first camera. You can see them in museums now. Gosh."

"Did he have any good ones, miss. I mean ones of here before now?"

"Here before now? Well, he hunted around, I know that. He's still full of energy, my grandfather. He said that he thought he had some stored in an album or tin can but no, he could not find them."

"Not one?"

"No. Over time, things get lost, mislaid, thrown away. If they didn't, we'd be drowning in our past, don't you think? That's why we have museums, to keep the most important things from the way we were."

Dilly was disappointed. She'd hoped to see an assortment of photos, clues to the way her new home had changed over time, and most of all proof that what she'd seen was true. As the days had gone by, she'd started to doubt it, but Simon was there in her memory, and that kept her focused.

"There was one thing," said Miss Roberts. "Grandpa

was a scientist by profession. Well, an engineer of some kind. Too clever for me by half. But he painted. Apparently, he started when he was about thirteen and carries on to this day, not so much of course, but it's admirable, don't you think? And he painted a picture of the view from his back window. He kept it because it was the first thing he ever painted at all."

"Have you seen it, miss?" Dilly asked.

"I have it," she said. "The wonders of modern technology. He asked a neighbour to scan it and they sent me the file. I have printed it and framed it for you."

Dilly's eyes opened wide. Teachers in her old school were conscientious, but Miss Roberts had gone above and beyond the call of duty. She took from behind her desk a package about the size of an A4 sheet of paper and unwrapped it. Inside was a print framed in dark wood. Miss Roberts gave it to Dilly saying, "Is this any use to you both?"

Dilly held the print and Laura stared at it over her shoulder. There before her was the exact landscape she'd somehow witnessed. There were the houses, the playground, the grass, the paths, the fence, the reservoir beyond. Miss Roberts's grandfather had done a good job, especially as he was so young at the time. It looked like it had been painted in watercolour – you could tell that even though it was a print. But the detail was there. It was unmistakeable. There was no chance that this scene could have been anywhere else, and Dilly knew it.

"Well?" Miss Roberts asked. "Is it useful?"

"It's perfect, miss. Perfect."

0000 0111: THE PAINTING

The print was propped up on the table, alongside her tablet. She kept staring at it, astonished that her new teacher should take the time and trouble to do this for her, then that her grandfather had painted it in the first place, and finally because she was desperate to see it again, to make sure she hadn't dreamt up the whole episode. It had, she thought, been painted with affection. She doubted that any painter would paint something they didn't like, so Grandfather Roberts must have liked this view, even if he and his family left soon after. Better that than seeing it all torn down for mountains of glass.

There was quite a lot of detail. You could see the colours on each front door and the flowers in rear balcony boxes on another block. The colours probably weren't accurate because it was a print, and even if it was the real thing, she doubted that the colours would be spot on. Nevertheless, you got a clear idea of how much care some of the families living there must have taken with their new homes. Miss Roberts had told her that it was just after the war and people were thankful to be alive and to have a place to live. It was, again Miss Roberts' words, a 'brave new world' and you could sense it in the freshness of the picture. Dilly would have liked to see the real painting. It had probably faded a bit by now, and whoever had scanned it had possibly deepened the colours, which was cheating, but an acceptable kind of cheating.

Some of the balconies, though small, had blooms of roses and other flowers, rich and happy, spilling over the sides. Dilly decided that she would try to do the same thing in her new home. The old and the new were chalk and cheese, but they had a balcony so there would be no harm growing flowers there. She would have to make sure they weren't sitting on the edge of the precipitous drop, but there was space to do something nice. She also wondered if they could paint their door, maybe pink or purple, like one or two in the picture. She doubted it. There were probably rules that prohibited doing anything not in keeping with the rest of the ghastly tower.

Then there was the playground in the distance. As far away as it was, you could see the see-saw, the swings, the roundabout, the slide and the sand. So many children had been using it, even at dusk, something almost impossible for Dilly to imagine. Were there no bad people around then? Had they all been born later? It made no sense. She touched the slide and the swings, hoping to make them move, but they were just flat prints. Even the sparkling reservoir water beyond the fence was visible. Dilly imagined it as she'd seen it, twinkling in the evening.

She picked up her mobile and called Laura.

"I keep looking at it, Laura," she said. "I so want to know that he's alright there."

"I'm sure he is," said Laura. "Maybe you'll get back there again."

"You still believe me?"

"Course I do! Why wouldn't I?"

"For a thousand reasons," said Dilly.

It was remarkable that Laura had proved such a trusting friend. Dilly hadn't told anyone else at the new school, she daren't. It was bad enough being labelled 'the girl who fainted' without adding 'nutty' to it, or 'the girl who time travelled'. Laura was totally at ease with what had happened, almost as if she had inside information and knew it to be true.

"Any sign of the mystery WiFi?" Laura asked.

"Nothing," said Dilly. "Not seen it once."

"Check it now," said Laura.

Dilly was taken aback.

"Should I?"

"I've got a feeling," said Laura.

Dilly moved Laura to the top right corner of her mobile and scrolled through the settings to the list of WiFi connections.

"Dilly?"

"I'm here."

"Well?"

"It's here, too."

Smack in the centre of the screen, flashing red, was

YpHi711172123275

"Spell it out," said Laura, "and tell me the numbers. I'll save it on my phone."

Dilly read out the name and the numbers. There was truly something familiar hidden, but she could not work out what it was. She sat up straight, wondering whether to touch it. She wasn't in the school playground but she didn't want her mum to find her on the floor. They would be at the hospital again, and this time they would keep her there.

"I'll come round," said Laura. "Don't tap it till I get there."

She got there in about twenty minutes, during which time Dilly paced around the room, looking first at the print then at her mobile, flashing away. What was going on, and why? Was Simon in so much trouble that he was somehow sending messages through time for help? She worried for him and wanted to help, even though she knew that some things you had to sort out yourself. In fact, most things you had to sort out yourself. Exactly who was getting the help here anyway? She was the one who'd been unhappy, she was the one who'd moved from Abi and the seaside to this comic book city with glass buildings touching the clouds.

She was the one who'd almost cried each night for weeks wanting to go home and cursing big money that was supposed to bring happiness but seemed to bring trouble instead. There was no answer, at least not an obvious one that she could see. Maybe Laura would see it.

The doorbell rang and Dilly was at the door well before her mother who popped her head around the lounge door saying hello to Laura then getting back to work.

"Let me see," said Laura, quietly.

Dilly showed her the flashing WiFi.

"It does feel urgent," she said.

"Doesn't it just," Dilly replied.

"Is it the same colour you saw when you were at school?"

"Exactly the same."

"And you haven't tapped it?"

"I'm scared to."

"You shouldn't be scared," said Laura. "Excited, maybe. I don't think that whatever is going on means any harm, do you?"

Dilly didn't think that at all, but what it did mean was baffling.

"Do you want to tap it?" she asked Laura.

"Gosh, no!" Laura answered. "I mean, I'm not scared, in fact I'd love to do it, I really would, but it's your phone and the message is for you."

"Is it a message, do you think?"

"It's an SOS, probably," said Laura. "Save Our Souls." Dilly looked puzzled. "That's what it means, SOS, and that's what this is, I believe."

Laura had an adult way of talking and even of behaving. Dilly liked it. Some of the other children had school took the mickey but Laura didn't notice. She was very sure of who she was and pretty sure of who the mickey takers were. She was unshakeable. If this close-to-magic phone didn't shake her, nothing would.

"An SOS from Simon?"

"Why not?"

That was what Dilly had been thinking. If it was, she shouldn't hesitate, she should just tap the connection and see what happened. If nothing happened, there would have to be a reason, but Dilly absolutely knew that something would happen. She felt the energy in the phone, more so than when she'd held it in the playground on the first day of school. The flashing red connection was full of implications. The thought that it was simply a bug in the software was nonsense. That was less believable than the possibility of time travel. Well, maybe not, but the bug idea was still nonsense. There was meaning and intention in the flashing message.

"If I faint, you won't tell anyone, will you?" Dilly asked her friend.

"No! Except your mum. Besides, you won't faint. You're ready for it this time. You're prepared."

"Am I? Maybe I'll end up somewhere else. If it's all in my head and not real, I could end up anywhere."

Laura picked up the print.

"Isn't this proof that it's not in your head, that it happened?"

It was truly odd the way things worked out, that Miss Roberts was her Head of House and pastoral carer, that her family had lived here and that she had the patience and generosity to follow up Dilly's request. Ninety-nine teachers out of a hundred would be too busy to help out, or wouldn't have known the area nor had a grandfather who painted it seventy years ago for heaven's sake. And here was Laura, a brand new friend, caring and generous and trusting, fully believing that something mysterious was going on.

"Should we make a plan?" Dilly asked.

"What kind of plan?" Laura asked.

"If I'm not back soon, what will you tell my mum?"

"I don't think it works like that. Last time, you didn't vanish for days, did you? Not even minutes. You were there the whole time. We all saw you. Here, sit in this chair, be comfy. I'll hold your hand. If you get pulled somewhere far away, I'll come with you, but you won't, not for real."

Dilly sat herself down and gripped the phone. The connection continued to flash. If it stopped, did that mean Simon had given up, or the phone had given up on her. It surely would not wait forever.

"I'm still scared," said Dilly.

"I would be, too," Laura replied, "and you don't have to tap it. Nothing will happen if you don't."

The thought passed through Dilly's mind to forget this whole silly business. Why did she have to tap this odd WiFi connection? She hadn't been asked to. The last time she did it, she had an upsetting experience. Next time it could be worse. It might be an electronic response test by the company that made the mobile phone. She'd heard of such things on television, countries bugging phones and mobiles doing strange things to your head. Maybe it was true, the mobile makers were experimenting with a new technology that made you see things when you tapped their secret link. That could be the answer. They'd built it into a handful of phones and were following the results on secret screens in secret rooms in secret places. That way, they could deny any knowledge of it. She wouldn't tap the wretched thing. She would ignore it and just get on with her new life and her new friend.

"Look!" Laura's voice was urgent as she pointed at the print.

It was fading!

"Laura, what's happening?"

Laura said, "It's probably showing you what will

happen if you don't tap it."

"But why? What has the picture got to do with anything?"

The picture was definitely fading. Pixel by pixel, it was disappearing from behind the glass. It was as if the artist that painted it never painted it at all and so it had no place any longer in Dilly's world. Or her teacher's world. All kinds of questions raced through Dilly's mind, and there were no obvious answers.

The flashing increased in speed and intensity. Dilly's heart beat faster. Laura squeezed her hand but did not press her to make a decision. This was Dilly's choice and hers alone.

"Whatever happens," said Laura, "I'm here."

"Whatever happens," Dilly repeated to herself, "whatever happens, whatev…" and she tapped the link.

0000 1000: ALONE AND AFRAID

Twilight. Simon sat in the undergrowth of brambles and prickles alongside the canal. It couldn't have been comfortable but he had his reasons. He picked at the leaves even though some of them hurt his fingers, even made one of them bleed. He pulled a face but kept doing it, as if tempting the world to make things even worse than they were, he didn't care. The bullies were winning. They'd probably won already. His cheek still hurt from where one of them had punched him and his left leg hurt from where one of them had kicked him. Most of all, he hurt inside because he had not kicked back or punched back. His mother hated violence. With the best love in the world, she'd covered him in kisses and hugs, but none of them healed the inner wound. And his father had had enough of it for a few lifetimes. He'd thought of asking his dad to come and look for them, to tell them off and make them never trouble him again, but he couldn't. His dad had fought in the biggest war ever. He was tired and quiet and wanted only to be home and at peace. Besides, Simon knew that his was his own battle. Even if his dad had sought out the bullies, it would not have helped the nagging feeling inside that he had to find an answer. So he came here where no one would find him to change himself. He had to. Even though he didn't know how, he had to think up a way to make himself feel better, to do the right thing. But he simply couldn't. He was locked in a prison of doubt and fear and the bullies had the key.

There were boys in his class who wouldn't have stood for it. They were fiercer and had different mums and dads, so they thought different and acted different. He wanted to be like them, but if he was, he would no longer be Simon.

Here, he was alone and quiet, the way he liked it. It wasn't necessarily safe as it was desolate and lonely, but Simon didn't care about any such fears. He was afraid of the bullies but not of this isolated undergrowth at twilight.

Until he heard a noise behind. The noise of squished leaves and a gentle moaning.

He jumped up and peered into the dusk.

"Dilly!"

"Is that you, Simon?"

"Course it is! You came back!"

"Did I?"

"You're here, aren't you?"

The Dilly ghost shook itself up unsteadily and took in the new surroundings.

"Where's here?"

"The canal and the reservoir. Near it, anyway."

"Not the basement?"

"No. You can see it isn't."

"Yes. Gosh, I feel strange."

The Dilly ghost swayed and tottered and then hovered over the nettles and prickles.

"I'd given up on you," said Simon. "I wanted you to come back, but you didn't."

"I didn't know how," said Dilly, "not completely. I can't explain, Simon, you have to trust me. How long ago was I here, when those horrid boys attacked us?"

"Weeks," said Simon.

"I was worried," said Dilly. "I thought they might have hurt you."

Simon blushed and mumbled, "They did."

"But you're okay?"

"Sort of."

"I'm sort of okay, too," said Dilly. "I feel a bit peculiar."

"Have you come a long way?" asked Simon.

"I haven't come any distance at all, I think," Dilly answered, "but still further than you can ever imagine."

"I can imagine lots," said Simon.

They tried to work out why the other was there. Simon was quietly delighted. He'd been wishing the Dilly ghost back. He liked her and for reasons that he couldn't explain, thought she could help him. Dilly, on the other hand, now she was here, wondered what she could possibly do to help this lonely, bullied boy.

"It's dark," she said, "darkish."

"I have to go home soon," said Simon. "I come here to think. It's quiet."

Dilly took in the wild landscape.

"It really is. Do your mum and dad know where you are?"

"They know where they think I am," said Simon. "I don't tell anyone where I really am. How did you find out?" The Dilly ghost shook its head. "I suppose ghosts have their way," Simon added.

"I told you last time, I'm not a ghost. This place," Dilly said, "you shouldn't come here alone. Anyone can see that. There could be…" she hesitated. Simon asked her what. "Just bad people. You must be brave or silly."

"Silly," said Simon.

Dilly sighed and inspected herself, seeing how much of her she could see.

"Am I still half visible?" she asked.

"I suppose because it's getting dark. I still have to squint, though. Can I try something?" he asked. The Dilly ghost agreed. "Hold me arm or my belt or some part of me," Simon said.

Dilly did so and immediately came into sharp focus. When she let go, she faded a little, but not completely.

"I thought it would work," Simon said. "It makes sense."

"Not to me," replied Dilly. "I'm glad you're alright, though" she added. "I thought... well, I thought horrible things."

"Did you?" Simon asked. "I mean, were you really worried?"

"Of course! I hate bullies. I don't know why they're here."

"They go to my school," said Simon.

"No, I mean why they are here, on Earth. What use are they? Just a waste of space."

Simon laughed.

"I wish I could tell them that."

"Are they still around, then?"

Simon nodded. Dilly looked closely at him.

"I can see bruises. It wasn't your dad, was it?"

Simon unexpectedly stamped his foot.

"I told you, my dad would never hurt me, never, never, never!"

"Only..."

"It was them, those boys."

Dilly looked at the bruises and touched Simon's arm in friendship. All he could feel was the brush of a feather and maybe a tiny pinprick of warmth.

"We'll have to deal with them, somehow."

Simon was taken aback. The Dilly ghost had said 'we' as if this was a joint job now.

"I'm not sure what a ghost can do," he said.

"I won't say it again," said Dilly, "I'm not a ghost. But perhaps I could frighten them if they saw me. You know, ooohs and aaahs and stuff."

Simon laughed again. He had such a lovely, light laugh, it just wasn't heard enough.

"I have to go home," he said. "Will you come with me again?"

"Some of the way," she answered.

Simon led her through the brambles and showed her the secret entrance, a tear in the wire that was supposed to stop vandals breaking in, although what kind of vandalism could be done to such a wild area was a mystery. Dilly looked around intently. She had in mind the picture that had faded just before she arrived. She wanted to see it, exactly as it was painted, but she couldn't remember exactly where it was.

"What are you looking for?" Simon asked.

"A scene," she said, "something I saw before I left, reminded me of you and here. It's somewhere around."

"Did you truly come back because of me?" Simon asked. The Dilly ghost nodded. "That was kind of you. Will you stay this time?"

"I don't know," said Dilly. "I didn't want to leave last time."

"You vanished when they came. I wondered why."

"So did I," said Dilly. "I didn't plan it. It just happened. If it happens again, don't think I'm doing it on purpose."

"You couldn't have done anything anyway. They're not afraid of anything, those boys."

"I bet they are," said Dilly. "That's why they're bullies. They're probably afraid of more than you think," which was indeed food for Simon's thoughts.

They came to the boundaries of the estate where children were still out playing, even at this time. Dilly couldn't believe it. In a way, she was a little jealous, maybe even a lot jealous. There was such a sense of freedom as if all the troubles in the world had faded. They hadn't, of course, Simon was proof of that, but it felt like a different planet. Simon trotted beside her, all of a sudden quite chatty.

"I'm glad you came back," he said again. "I don't understand what's going on, but you make me feel better." Dilly was delighted to hear that, but she didn't like the idea of Simon struggling to face the enemy alone. "You make me feel special," he added, "even though you're the special one. I mean, you found a way here, to help me, from wherever you came from. I was wishing you back. Perhaps I didn't wish hard enough. I wished all day and night, but you never came."

"I told you, it isn't easy," said Dilly. "The moment has to be right."

"How do you do it?" Simon asked, ever the enquiring mind.

Just like before, Dilly didn't know how to explain. There would be so many words Simon wouldn't understand, it would take forever, and he'd be none the wiser. She said that it was something she was trying to work out herself.

When they reached Simon's home, his mother was knitting and his father was filling in a newspaper crossword. His mother greeted him with a hug and a kiss; his father nodded and asked him for five letter word meaning a perambulator. Simon had no idea. "Buggy," his father said. "You should try crosswords, son, they're good for the brain."

Dilly stood there, embarrassingly invisible to them as she had been to all the people they'd passed walking back. She gripped Simon's arm for dear life, as if letting go would make her invisible to the entire universe, for ever. She had a vision of floating away into a terrible void, never being able to return.

"Would you like a cocoa, darling?" his mother asked.

He hesitated before saying he was going to do some homework first.

"Come on," he whispered to Dilly.

"What was that?" his father asked.

"Oh, nothing, dad."

"First sign of madness," his father said, "talking to

76

yourself."

When Simon moved, he suddenly jerked back. Dilly was pulling him towards the balcony of the sitting room. To his parents, it looked as though he was playing the fool.

"Simon," his mother joked, "have you been drinking."

He shook his head and hurried towards the balcony, both parents eyeing him curiously. Dilly pulled him anxiously to see what she could see through the balcony window. She'd seen it last time, but it hadn't registered. Now it did. It was the scene in the painting, clear as daylight. It was probably similar from many of the balconies in the blocks on the estate, with a slightly different angle, but for the moment, this was it.

"It was fading when I left," she said.

"What was?" Simon asked.

"What was what?" his mother said.

His father looked up and asked Simon again if he was alright.

"Fine," said Simon, "I was thinking something and I spoke it out loud."

Dilly was fixated on the scene, half expecting it to disappear just as the print had started to vanish, but it remained.

"I need to talk to you," she whispered

"Yes," he replied.

"Yes what?" his father asked. "My boy, you are behaving strangely, you know that, don't you?"

Dilly pulled Simon through to his room as his parents looked on, his mother especially staring hard. Simon sank down on his bed.

"It's extraordinarily difficult you being invisible to them," he said. "Can you make them see you?"

"I can't make anything happen," said Dilly. "I'm as much in the dark as you."

"But we aren't in the dark."

"Well, the lights are bright. I can't explain it, Simon."

She'd let go of his arm and became a half visible form again, as long as he half closed his eyes.

"Where I came from," she said," there was this picture. A painting. It was done by my teacher's grandfather. She gave it to me. To show me what it used to be like where I live."

Simon scratched his head.

"How did he get it?" he asked.

"He did it," Dilly explained. "He used to live here, too, like you. And it's important." Simon asked why. "I don't know for sure, but it started to fade when I was deciding whether to come here or not."

"Deciding?"

"Yes. I had to decide, Simon. I was scared."

"Were you?" he asked "Ghosts are supposed to scare other people, not get scared themselves."

"That might be true, but I'm not a ghost, for the hundredth time. Do you know any children at school who can paint?"

"Lots of them," said Simon. "Why were you scared, Dilly?"

Dilly turned her pale face towards Simon.

"I didn't know what was going to happen. I might have died!"

Simon thought that this was the same feeling he had when the bullies attacked him, so he sympathised, even though he couldn't see in his mind's eye how the Dilly ghost's situation was in any way similar.

"Perhaps you did die," he dared to say, "and this is your ghost."

The thought had occurred to Dilly, too, but she'd been here before, and you only died once, not twice. Besides, she felt quite well and alive, not a bit dead, despite appearances.

Their talk was interrupted by a hesitant knocking on the

bedroom door. It was such a quiet tap, tap, tap that both of them thought it had to be Simon's mother, but no, the door opened slightly and Simon's father poked his head inside.

"Can I come in for a chat, son?"

"Oh, erm, well…"

"Jolly good," said his father, came in and closed the door behind. Dilly didn't know whether to sneak out whilst the door was open but by the time she'd made up her mind, it was too late. Unless… she recalled that ghosts were able to move through doors as well as walls and other solid objects, but she couldn't risk it, not now. If it went wrong and there was a thud and Simon's dad witnessed it, heaven knew what might happen. So she backed away into a corner and waited to see what Simon's father wanted.

"Son, mum and I have wanted to talk to you for a while about something important."

Simon feared the worst. They were going to ask him about the bullying and open up a big can of worms.

"Everything's alright, dad, really," said Simon, glancing at Dilly who was standing as still as a statue in the corner. His father looked where he was looking, saw nothing and turned back to his son.

"One day, when you grow up, you'll have to have the same talk with your son, and believe me, it isn't easy."

For some reason, Dilly knew exactly what Simon's father was about to explain, and she looked up to the heavens, or at least the bedroom ceiling. She wished she'd escaped the room a minute before.

"Could we do it another time, dad?" Simon asked.

"No time like the present, son. Never do today what you can put off till tomorrow, eh? Ha ha! Now. You're going to be a young man soon, not a boy."

Dilly wanted to dissolve into the air, even more than she already was half dissolved. She willed Simon to argue the point and delay this important talk for another day. And yet, part of her was intrigued.

"I suppose so," said Simon.

"And all kinds of things go on inside your body."

Simon had noticed a few things lately, he had to admit, but now was not the time to discuss them, not with the Dilly ghost in the corner standing there, eyes wide open, looking highly uncomfortable.

"Son, are you listening? You keep looking over into the corner. Are you hiding something?"

Simon was tempted to say, 'Only a girl from the future' but wisely, he didn't, and just shook his head.

"Good," said his father, "now these changes are quite normal. They happen when a boy becomes a man. And by the way, they also happen when a girl becomes a woman."

Dilly stifled a laugh as Simon glanced at her in desperation.

"This is perfectly as it should be," said his father. "But with these changes come... how shall I say... desires. Do you know what that means?"

Simon was in shock. He'd expected a talk about bullying or schoolwork but this? It threw him completely, and he did not want the Dilly ghost there laughing at him.

"Not really, no, dad, but I can look it up in the encyclopaedia."

"Not everything can be learned from books, son. You're a clever boy and we love you for that. Mum and I are proud of you. I know I can be a bit bad tempered sometimes, but I love you very much and don't want you to be unhappy. There's no need for unhappiness. The world has had enough unhappiness for ever."

"No, dad, so..."

"And these changes can make you unhappy if you don't understand them."

He went into a long explanation of how a boy becomes a man and what it all meant for the future of the human race. Simon did his best to listen, and indeed, some of it was interesting, but he didn't feel quite ready for it, and this was absolutely the wrong time with the Dilly ghost wide eyed, fighting giggles in the corner of his room.

"If you're unhappy because of these changes," his father went on, "we don't want you to be. You should *not* be," he said, emphasizing the 'not'. "All boys and girls go through these stages, and so for that matter, do all animals. That's the way the world turns, isn't it? The thing is to understand, as it is with everything in life. Knowledge is power, Simon, so knowing this will let you deal with it in a sensible way."

"Yes, dad. I think I ought to get on with my homework now."

"In a moment," and he continued with a few examples of how he had dealt with some of the changes when he was a boy. Dilly put fingers in her ears but being only half there, it had only half the effect and she heard everything. Simon wanted to do the same. In fact, he would have given anything to slip through the floorboards into a different dimension, like the Dilly ghost. "Now," his father ended, "if you ever want to ask me anything... anything at all... don't be shy. I repeat, Simon, don't be shy. There's nothing to be shy about in these matters, nothing at all." Simon wanted to believe him but somehow his father had seemed shy right the way through his long explanation. "I'm proud of you, son," his father ended. "You're the best of boys."

Simon didn't feel like it. His head was spinning with everything his father had said, very little of which had stuck, but most of all the embarrassment of knowing the Dilly ghost had heard it all.

"Well," he said to her once his father had left, "say it."

"Say what?"

"I don't know. Say anything."

Dilly simply laughed out loud, which made Simon even more embarrassed, so he laughed, too.

"They don't really know what's going on at all, do they?" she asked.

"How do you mean?"

"About the bullying."

It was true. They suspected that Simon was unhappy about something but didn't know how serious it was. Instead, they thought it was a birds and bees problem and his father had tried to solve it with a gentle talk about the subject.

"I'm not sure I want to talk about it, either," said Simon.

"They're rubbish," said Dilly.

"What, my parents?"

"No, silly, those bullies. Your parents are sweet. The question is what to do about them."

"There's nothing I can do," said Simon.

Dilly wanted so much to help. Simon was a terrific boy with lots of ideas and interests, she knew that at once, and especially after seeing his room with so many books and posters and the fish tank with happy goldfish still chasing each other. It was wrong that he should suffer like this at the hands of thugs. She knew the world was not perfect, that bad things happened to good people and even that good things happened to bad people. She saw that bullying touched nations where harsh and thuggish leaders led their people into all kinds of troubles. She couldn't change that, but she could maybe help one boy.

"There's always something," she said, "the question is what."

Simon had moved over to his fish tank, tapping the glass and then dropping a little food into the water.

"I don't hate those boys," he said. "I just wish they'd disappear."

"You mustn't let them get to you."

"They already have. I can't stop it."

"Well, you have to get it out of you somehow otherwise

you won't grow up properly."

Simon looked at the Dilly ghost wondering how she was so wise and, still, why she was there, not to mention how she was there.

"I'll grow up alright," he said.

"I hope so," said Dilly, "but it must be like a poison inside you. We have to get it out."

Simon was secretly delighted that she said 'we' as if it was her problem as well as his. A problem shared is a problem solved, his mother had once old him. It wasn't necessarily totally true all the time, but there was truth in it. "Even if we do nothing, you have to end up feeling good about yourself."

Simon didn't reply. He did not feel good about himself. He did not know how to feel good about himself. There was one way, he suspected, but he did not know if he could do it. And he did not know if it was right. His mother had cuddled him to pieces and his father was quietly suffering from all that happened in the war so this was up to him. He trusted the Dilly ghost even though he did not know her, but could she tell him what to do or would he have to decide for himself?

"Why are you interested?" He asked her.

"Because I'm here," she said. "I don't like wrong things happening. Do you?"

"No, of course not."

"Besides," she added, "I like you."

Simon looked surprised. He hadn't made any good friends since they'd moved here but he liked the Dilly ghost, even though she was only half real. He wished she could somehow fix herself and stay for good. They would make excellent friends.

"I like you, too," he said self-consciously, "at least the bit I can see."

Their laughter was interrupted by another knock at the

door.

"Oh no," said Simon, "not another speech."

This time, his mother poked her head around the door.

"I heard you laughing," she said, "are you alright?" she asked, as if laughing were a sign of something amiss.

"Fine mum, everything's alright."

"Only laughing alone is a little odd, Simon."

"I thought of something funny, that's all."

"Can I come in and chat anyway?"

"Well…"

"I won't be long," his mother said and came in, looking around, as if suspicious that he was hiding something or someone away, which of course he was.

"Daddy told me that he'd had a little chat with you so I won't do the same."

Simon waited. The less he said, the sooner his mum would go, he hoped. Dilly stood in the corner again, wondering what she would hear this time. She desperately hoped it wasn't another birds and bees talk. His mother continued:

"Is there anything you couldn't ask daddy that you can ask me, Simon?"

Oh, oh, thought Dilly and Simon.

"No, absolutely nothing, mum."

"Because you can ask either of us, or both of us. We're all grown ups, and so are you, Simon, nearly."

"Yes, mum."

"Because I was thinking that when we moved here a few months ago, you didn't really want to come, did you?"

"I didn't mind."

"Moving home is not easy. You never know what you are letting yourself in for, but this is a nice home, isn't it? You're happy here?"

"I am, mum."

"If you're not, all you have to do is tell us why."

"I will."

"You don't seem happy, Simon, I have to say that. You look distinctly unhappy sometimes. That's why I asked daddy to come and speak with you. We thought it might be, you know, growing up pains. Is it?" It wasn't. "Dad didn't really want to do it so I thought I'd better come and check that you were okay and that there's nothing else bothering you. School's alright?" It was and it wasn't, but Simon refused to tell his mother what was happening. "We can speak to the teachers if you're finding it hard, although you're a clever boy, cleverer than your dad and I, at least."

His mother laughed and ruffled Simon's hair.

In the corner, Dilly saw how much Simon was loved and cared for but also how caged up he was, not knowing how to unlock the cage and break free.

"It wouldn't be easy to move home again," said Simon's mother, "I have to be honest. There were lots of people wanting to move here. We were lucky. It wouldn't look good asking to move again. The council would wonder why, and so would we. You don't want to move, do you, Simon?"

He didn't. What was going on there could go on anywhere, even if they moved to the moon. And his mum was right, it was a lovely place to live. If only he could make friends and be rid of his enemies. Dilly seemed to read his mind. She ventured forward.

"Oh!" exclaimed Simon's mother.

Dilly froze.

"What, mum?" Simon asked.

His mother looked around, puzzled.

"I thought... I thought I saw something."

"Shadow, probably," Simon said.

"Probably," said his mother looking slightly agitated. She focused her eyes on her son again. "Where was I?"

"Asking me if I wanted to move again, and I don't."

Dilly thought this was quite brave. Considering that he was scared to death a lot of the time, he could have told his mum and dad that he hated home and school and wanted to go back. But unlike Dilly, Simon hadn't come from the seaside, they'd moved from an old dilapidated house that needed to be demolished. Their new home and his new school was Paradise in comparison. It would make no sense to leave it.

"I believe you, Simon, you know that. But I think you're hiding something from me. I wish you could open your heart and tell me."

Dilly wanted to intervene and explain what Simon couldn't explain. It was all she could do to keep silent. Simon sat, looking down one moment, then glancing at Dilly the next. Once again, his mother glanced to where he was looking and frowned.

"I think I need to see the optician," she whispered. Simon looked up, asking a question with his expression. "It's just that…"

"What, mum?"

"Oh, nothing, silly me, Simon. My eyes play tricks on me. I'm getting old."

Dilly played statues, even trying not to breathe.

"You're not old, mum. You're still pretty."

His mother laughed out loud.

"I wish," she said, and gave her son a big hug. "Is there anything you'd like, as a present, I mean, something to cheer you up?"

Simon had a think.

"I wouldn't mind a painting set?"

The talk with Dilly had given him an idea, and when Simon had an idea, he had to follow it up.

"Really?" said his mother. "I thought you were more a science boy!"

"I am," said Simon, "and I want to be a scientist.

Honest. But I'd like to paint. We do painting at school and I'm quite good at it. It wouldn't be anything expensive."

"I'll talk to daddy about it. I'm sure we can find something. That's a surprise, Simon, but a nice one. I used to paint when I was girl, did you know that? You didn't, of course, I've never told you, but I did. I won a prize at school. I would have liked to have been an artist but I'm too busy for art nowadays," she laughed, although it was a laugh tinged with regret. This wasn't just Simon's mother, it was a woman who had had ideas and talents, perhaps, all brought to an end by a terrible war and the call of duty, to country and to home. They were too young to imagine the full story, but Dilly especially saw something sensitive and hidden inside Simon's loving mother. Maybe that was why she sensed Dilly more than Simon's father. "A paint box! Well, well, well!" whispered his mother. "Who would have... oh!"

Dilly had moved towards Simon, unable to keep still for so long. To Simon's mother, it was as if a breeze had drifted across the room. She looked up, blinked and screamed.

Footsteps were heard outside and the door burst open. Simon's father rushed in, held his wife by the arm and took in the scene. Simon was open eyed with shock and his mother was open eyed with fear, pointing at the wall. Simon's father stared at where she was pointing but saw nothing except the wall.

"What is it, my love?" he asked, glancing at Simon as if it was his fault.

"A ghost!" she whispered.

Simon's father screwed up his face and said to his wife.

"A ghost, my love? Are you serious?"

"I saw it," she said, "a girl, shimmering away there, near our son. This place is haunted, Peter, haunted."

Simon's father breathed out.

"Poppycock," he said. He was not a believer at all in

such things. He was as down to Earth as it is possible to be, almost stuck in it, and he had no time for such nonsense. "What are you saying, my dear. Come on, calm down."

His wife was visibly shaken, in fact she was still shaking.

"I saw her, clear as day. Well, almost. She was transparent, Peter. I could see through her. A girl, our Simon's age. Standing there, looking at me."

Simon dreaded his father asking him whether or not he had seen anything himself because he would have to lie and he was a bad liar. Luckily, his father was so sure this was untrue that he didn't even consider verifying it.

"My dear, my love," he said, "do calm down. There is nothing here, nothing at all. There are no ghosts, no spirits, no whatsits at all. Look. Nothing."

Simon's mother looked around.

"It's gone," she said.

"It was never here," said Simon's father. "Goodness, woman, you scared the daylights out of me."

"I saw it," his wife insisted, "I swear on my life."

"Now, now," said her husband, "no swearing, not on something like this. Open your eyes again, you won't see anything except our son all shaken up because of your screaming."

Simon's mother grabbed Simon, saying, "Are you alright, Simon, did it hurt you? You must have been terrified!"

Simon looked at his father but said nothing.

"Don't scare the boy, Mary," his father said. "He's fine. He's more frightened of your screaming than any ghosts. My goodness, what a palaver."

"It isn't a palaver, Peter, I saw something. It may have gone now, but it was there. I don't know why you can't believe me."

"I can't believe you because I don't believe in the

heebie-jeebies, Mary. You've been a bit overwrought, lately, maybe it was tiredness, or a trick of the light. These things happen."

"No they don't, Peter. These things don't happen. That's just it, they don't, but it did. You won't get me to change my mind. This house is haunted."

"How can it be haunted, dearest? We are the first people to live in it! It's only a year old. Look, I can't explain but all is well, trust me."

Simon's mother cuddled Simon but would not be calmed. She had seen what she had seen and nothing would dissuade her from that. She was loathe to leave her son alone in the room.

"I'm alright, mum, honest," said Simon.

"Oh, my brave boy."

"There's nothing here," he said, which was absolutely true.

The Dilly ghost had vanished.

0000 1001: ELEPHANT IN THE ROOM

Dilly sat up sharply. She was still holding Laura's hand.

"Are you alright, Dilly?" Laura asked.

She blinked, looking around at her familiar room and her friend.

"It happened," she said.

"No time at all has passed here," said Laura, "not a minute."

"Truly?"

"You closed your eyes and opened them again. That's all."

Dilly shook her head. Was there something wrong with her? She felt okay, a bit shaken by what had happened, or what she thought had happened, but that was all.

"His mother saw me," she said.

"Who, Simon's?"

"She screamed. I nearly fainted, but I suppose you can't faint if you're already in a faint, can you?"

"I don't think you fainted, Dilly."

"No?"

"No. But I believe you." Dilly gripped her friends' hand. "Look," said Laura.

She pointed at her grandfather's painting. It was there, solid as before, not fading, not vanished. Dilly let go of Laura's hand and held the framed print, staring at it intently.

"I saw it, almost exactly the same," she said, "outside his window."

"Simon's?"

"Yes. Then his mother came in and saw me, Laura, she saw me. His dad didn't. He came in, too, but I was invisible to him. Not to her, though. She screamed like she'd seen a ghost."

"She had," said Laura.

"What's going on?" Dilly asked.

Before Laura could answer, there was a knock on the bedroom door. For a moment, Dilly thought she was back in Simon's room and that his mother or father would come in, but it was her own mother.

"Everything alright?" she asked.

Dilly snapped out of her daze. The last thing she wanted was to be taken back to the hospital.

"Course it is, mum," said Dilly.

Her mother was about to leave when she saw the print.

"That's lovely," she said, coming over and picking it up to take a closer look, "what is it?"

"It's here," said Dilly, "a long time ago."

Her mother examined the picture, impressed.

"It's very good. Who did it?"

"Miss Roberts' grandfather. He painted it when he was a boy. They used to live here, mum, and that's what it looked like then."

"I'd say early 1950s," her mother guessed, "is that right?"

"Just after the coronation of Queen Elizabeth," said Dilly.

Her mother laughed. It seemed such an exact and strange thing for her daughter to say.

"I was born in the year of the silver jubilee," she said, "twenty-five years after all this. How the world has changed! How this place has changed! Let me see. Ah, yes, the water, that looks similar."

"It wasn't a boating lake then, mum," said Dilly, "it was a reservoir. They needed water for the estate."

"And how do you know that, Dilly?"

Dilly blushed. Laura came to her aid.

"We're doing it as a project, Mrs Paget. Studying local history."

"And your teacher's family used to live here? That's a coincidence, isn't it. Is this a playground?" she added.

"A nice one," said Dilly, "but a bit dangerous. It's all hard."

"Hard? You mean the ground is, what, gravel? Brick? Difficult to tell from the painting. Did your teacher tell you that, too?"

Dilly had noticed this at the time. The playground surface was stone hard. You wouldn't want to fall off a swing or roundabout onto that.

"When I was a girl," her mother reminisced, "these kind of places started to disappear. He captured everything, didn't he, the painter? You can even see the wood grains on the see saw. How old was he when he did this?"

Dilly wasn't sure. Maybe thirteen, fourteen.

"Well, he's probably a famous artist by now. Lots of talent. You can see that. The more I look, the more I see. There are glints of sunlight in the water, reflections on the metal in the bars, cracks in the bricks – my goodness, he must have loved it to paint in such detail. I bet the original is even clearer. Very clever. Ah, girls, how quickly time flies."

She sat herself down on a chair and was quiet, lost in her own thoughts. For a moment, Dilly saw her own mother as a girl, playing outside with friends. How did she turn into a 'mum'? What happened to people when they grew up? Did they change, like butterflies from caterpillars?

Although she was doing her best to concentrate, Dilly's mind was only half on what she was saying. The other half was remembering what had just happened and trying to hold herself together. She took the picture back and pointed to the water at the back.

"You couldn't walk along the bank, then," she said, "it

was blocked off. There was a fence, a wire fence, and inside was all overgrown. There were nettles and stingers and long grasses. Nobody knew what to do with it so they fenced it off, but there were holes where the wire had rusted so you could go through if you were brave enough. It stretched for a long way so you could maybe get lost in all that long grass, but people did it anyway. If you wanted to be alone, you could be alone there. I saw all kinds of flowers. I don't know their names, but there were loads of colours. I'm pretty sure there were daisies and cow parsley, but that's all I know. I should really learn more. Next time, I'll recognise them and tell him. But it was lovely. I mean, it's nice now, with the path, but it was wild then, now it's all cut and tame. I don't care for it so much. I'd rather it was like it used to be…"

Dilly's mother was staring at her daughter, somewhat impressed, mostly anxious.

"Goodness, darling, you sound like you've actually been there."

"Oh yes," Dilly replied without thinking, even though Laura was urging her with her eyes to stop. "And the playground – you're right, it was stone and hard and very dangerous. There were no grown-ups there, either. They were allowed, but they didn't go. The children played all by themselves and it was alright. I think I saw one grown up, like a caretaker, in case of an accident, but it didn't seem to matter. Accidents happen, don't they. No, there were loads of children, on the roundabout and the swing and the slide. The slide looked fantastic, but you had to be careful not to fall off the end because it was stone or gravel not sand or grass. I didn't try it but next time I will. I'm a bit old but I think I'd be alright. I liked the swings, too, they were made of wood and you could go high but you had to hold on tight in case you fell and that would be bad because it was gravel, yes, I'm sure it was gravel. Simon said he had an accident there once but everyone has accidents and it wasn't that that frightened him, it was them, the bullies, the rotten, stinking bullies...."

"Dilly?"

Her mother had listened in increasing alarm but Dilly had not finished.

"The air was different, too. I wish I could explain. They'd had to do a lot of building like now, but it was different. They weren't so high and you could see more. You could see the sky, mum, lots of it, all over the reservoir and even further. It would have been like heaven, but it wasn't, because there were bad boys, really bad, and I left him there, and his mum saw me and his dad got angry and..."

"Dilly, darling," her mum interrupted, "stop now! Calm down. Look, you're all of a sweat and getting yourself worked up. Laura, did anything happen?"

Laura shook her head. What could she say? She hadn't seen anything, she simply trusted her friend. Unless it was more than that, but no one could tell from her expression. Laura had the face of an angel.

"I think it's being new here, that's all. She's still upset."

Dilly's mother wasn't convinced. People moved all the time. They got used to new homes and new places to live. They didn't go into blue funks like this. She felt Dilly's forehead which was hot and asked Laura to fetch some water from the kitchen.

"Come on, Dilly my love, pull yourself together and calm down. You have such an imagination!"

"I didn't imagine it, mum."

"Alright, I won't argue now." Laura returned and gave Dilly the water. "Sip it. That's right. I'll wipe your head. Good. I'm going to call the doctor."

"No, mum," Dilly insisted, "I'm fine, honestly. I got carried away with a story I'm making up about our project.

Isn't that right Laura?"

Laura nodded but said nothing more. Dilly was trying to calm herself but her head was burning with the vivid memories of what had happened, or what she thought had happened. No – definitely – what had definitely happened. She had been there again, in some form or other. It felt as real as anything she could see now in her new home with her mum and her best friend close by. She remembered Simon's mother's scream, the fact that she saw her when only Simon was supposed to see her. How did that happen? She was supposed to help, not to make things worse.

"Laura, stay with her for a while. I'll heat up some warm milk and make something to eat. That will help."

When they were alone, Laura said, "You got carried away, Dilly."

"I know. Although, I didn't know at the time. Sorry."

"You're all hot and bothered."

"I left Simon in a pickle. I keep leaving him when things go wrong. Oh, Laura, I wish I knew what was happening."

Laura was a dreamy girl herself, but she never got so lost in thoughts that she got lost in reality, too. She was too smart for that. She liked her new friend very much and didn't want Dilly's mother to think she was a bad influence - too much daydreaming, leading Dilly astray and so on. She was to blame in other ways, more important ways, but neither of them knew that, and now was not the time to tell.

"I wish I could do something," she said. "I kind of prompted you to tap the connection."

"I would have done it, anyway," said Dilly. "That's the key," she added. "That's what's taking me back, that WiFi. It isn't WiFi at all, is it, it's something dangerous. I should show mum, or Miss Roberts, or the police."

"Honestly, I don't think it's dangerous, Dilly. If it was, you'd know for sure. We always think things are dangerous if we don't understand them. Maybe it's a… a gift." Dilly asked what she meant. "A special way of helping someone in trouble. And helping you, too."

"Helping me! How is it helping me?"

"You've moved home. You don't like it, you're unhappy. But it's not that bad, Dilly. There are lots of good things, too."

"I suppose. But I won't feel happy until I know Simon's alright. What will he tell his mother? How will he explain me? And he's still got to fight those bullies."

"Fight them? Do you think he will? Do you think he can?"

Dilly didn't have any answers. She was trying to calm down, but all her thoughts were of getting back to help Simon and make both of them feel better about life. She was grateful to have Laura on her side. There was no reason she should be. Laura had held Dilly's hand when she'd made the leap and knew that no time at all had passed, yet still believed that something real and important had happened. That was special.

Her mother returned with two glasses of warm milk and some sandwiches.

"For you, too, Laura, you've been sweet to Dilly."

She watched the girls eat and drink with a worried expression. Clearly, her daughter was not well, or at least, something was bothering her.

"That's nice, mum, thanks."

"How are you feeling?" her mum asked, touching her forehead.

"Fine. Like I said, I get carried away."

"I used to get carried away, too," her mum said, "when I was a girl, a hundred years ago. But not like this, Dilly. Did you faint again? Laura, did she?"

"No, she didn't, Mrs Paget. I would have called you. I didn't see anything happen hear at all."

That was not a lie. Laura had seen nothing.

"That doesn't mean nothing happened," said Dilly's mother. "In here," she said, tapping Dilly's head. "So much goes on there that no one sees, isn't that right, my love?"

Dilly wanted to tell her mum everything but daren't. She doubted that her mother would be as trusting as Laura. Grown ups simply did not believe as easily. As loving and caring as her mother was, how could she believe in the impossible, because that was what this was. Impossible. You could not visit the past, let alone do it without time passing in the here and now. But that was what Dilly believed had happened. Was she mad? Was Laura being too good a friend?

"I used to write poems," said Dilly's mother. "Hundreds of them. I was in a world of my own. Do you believe that, girls? I don't think any of them were any good, but I had so much going on inside, I had to express it somehow."

"What were they about?" Laura asked.

"Everything. Nothing."

"Do you still have them, mum?"

"No. They're lost in time, like everything is, darling. You can't recapture the past."

Which was precisely what Dilly was doing.

"If you could," she said, "would you change it?"

Her mother thought for a moment.

"I might not have moved here. Sorry, Laura, it's lovely that Dilly has met you, but I can see that she's unhappy. We could move back, Dilly, it you're really unhappy."

Dilly gave this sudden but considerable thought, then shook her head. She'd met Laura who was patient, trusting and kind. She'd known Abi ever since they were children but Abi had been jealous. And there were other things happening, other possibilities. Besides, she wouldn't have told Simon to run away, so how could she? She felt intuitively that moving back would be wrong. There were hints that things were beginning to change, more than hints, she believed, when she saw Laura sitting by her side, all anxious and concerned.

Yet there was the elephant in the room. Dilly didn't know the expression, but she would have understood it. A massive presence they all felt but could not discuss. If they'd known it, they would have been aware of a thousand elephants, so many big things bubbling away in their heads which they couldn't share. This one was absolutely in the room with them - Dilly's all consuming obsession with the way things used to be and her imagined friend, Simon. That was how her mother saw it. An elephant, maybe, but what it truly was, none of them knew for sure.

"Perhaps give the school project a rest for a bit," said Dilly's mother.

For a second, neither of the girls knew what she meant, but then they recalled the little white lie. Dilly nodded. As there wasn't a project, it could rest easily enough. Dilly's mother suggested that Dilly give the internet a rest, too. "Just for a day or two."

Giving the internet a rest for most people would be like solitary confinement in the Tower of London. Dilly was no exception, even though she loved her books. Besides, she had an idea, to talk with the company that had given her the free mobile phone. If anyone could tell her what the YpHi connection meant, they would. She evaded the real reason by telling her mother that there were some technical thing she wanted to ask the company. Her mother looked puzzled.

"What technical things, Dilly?"

Dilly already knew that she was the world's worst liar. Even the simplest pretences unravelled within seconds. Little holes dug with fibs immediately became bottomless pits. She said that it didn't matter, she and Laura would sort it out. She had to find out what the flashing WiFi connection meant, and how it got there. Surely the best person to ask – the only people to ask - would be the mobile phone company. They could call them, but how would you explain such a thing to an employee, probably in a far off land, who would have less than no idea what you were talking about.

"You are a mystery, Dilly," said her mother, "but I love you for it. Your forehead is cooler now. Are you sure you're okay?" She was. "You don't want me to call the doctor?" She definitely did not. "Alright. Now, I've made something for us, to remind us of what happened. I didn't know whether to show it to you because, well, you're still not sure it was a good thing, I understand that. But it happened, Dilly, and we have to make it a good thing. Millions and millions of people dream of this. We have to make it work. What's the point of dreaming if you're unhappy when they come true."

"What is it?" Dilly asked.

Laura asked if she should go. This seemed like a private family chat.

"No, no," said Dilly's mother. "Wait. I'll get it."

Dilly had no idea what her mother could have made. She was an artist and could turn her hand to most things creative. So it was no surprise that what she had made was unique. She fetched it from her office, hoping Dilly would like it.

It was a framed design fronted with glass, about twenty centimetres long and ten high. The frame was white wood while the design, on a cerulean blue felt background showed a series of numbers embroidered in various coloured threads, separated by stars of golden yarn. It was stunning.

"Don't you recognise them, Dilly?"

She did, but maybe not just in the way her mother imagined. She didn't know whether to laugh or cry. All she did was squeeze Laura's hand.

"I thought I'd stand it on the mantlepiece. To remind us how lucky we we've been."

"It's very pretty," said Laura. "Does it mean anything?"

She might have asked innocently but there was a hint that she already knew the answer. This did not register with Dilly who was staring at her mother's creation.

"They're the numbers mum picked for the lottery when we won," whispered Dilly.

They were also a more familiar set of numbers. She wondered if Laura would recognise them, too. She didn't have to worry.

"Oh," whispered Laura, "aren't they…" then she paused, knowing that she should say no more. Again, there was a hint of knowledge that Dilly and her mother missed.

"Yes, they are," Dilly interrupted.

"Aren't they, what, Laura?"

"So pretty," Laura said.

They were indeed pretty, but for Dilly it was like unlocking the most secret code ever devised because the numbers her mother had sewn onto the felt were:

7 * 11 * 17 * 21 * 23 * 27 * 5

0000 1010: LUCKY NUMBERS

They were the same numbers shown on the misbehaving mobile connection:

YpHi711172123275

No wonder it didn't trip lightly off the tongue or be easily remembered. How strange. How bizarre. How absolutely peculiar. Could it be a coincidence? No way. What were the chances that the twelve digits of one should match the same as the twelve digits in their lottery numbers? About a billion billion to one. There was more chance of them winning the lottery a second time than that. No, this was connected and Dilly had to find the connection. Thank goodness for Laura. If it hadn't been for Laura, she would have had to do this totally alone, which would have been impossible. Now she had a friend to talk with and it was… well, it might still be impossible but they would endeavour to figure it out. If there was a mind behind all this, and surely there was, it probably wanted them to keep hunting rather than meekly give up.

Dilly tried a few times to contact the company that had given her the mobile. She was invariably met by a long list of button pressing options, none of which said, 'Press 1 if you want to find out about the mysterious flashing WiFi connection on your phone that transports you into the past. Press zero to return to the main menu.' Laura kept her company as much as possible, all the while looking rather uncomfortable.

"It shouldn't be this hard, should it?" Dilly asked.

They'd cheated once and pressed the button for sales. They got through straight away to a real, live person, but that person could not help. 'You need to press options 1 and 2', they'd said. Dilly had argued as best she could, but the lady at the other end was a touch impatient and insisted they go through the correct options. It was no good Dilly telling anyone that she simply wanted to speak with the same engineer who'd fitted out their home, that made no sense to anyone at the other end of the line at all. They tried looking at the company's Frequently Asked Questions.

"There's a lot of them," said Dilly.

They scrolled through pages and pages of FAQs which seemed to cover every possible problem, but not Dilly's.

"I guess it isn't frequently asked," she said.

"Never, probably," said Laura.

Then they tried the help forums from 'Your friendly community'. They had to register with a username and password and once again scroll through various forum boards each with a million questions from the simplest, 'How do I switch on my laptop?' to the most complex which might as well have been written in Martian. Once again, there was nothing about apparently magic WiFi connections, nor about tracing individual engineers. They got some rude responses from a couple of not so friendly members of the friendly community who thought they were wasting precious time and asking daft questions. 'Just call them, choose the option for faults and book a visit. Simples,' said one who then vanished.

"Can I do that without telling mum?" Dilly asked.

She couldn't. There was nothing wrong with their service except that it opened up some kind of wormhole into the past, and Dilly doubted that any engineer would be able to fix that.

"Except the one who gave me the mobile," said Dilly.

Once again, Laura looked uncomfortable.

"I'm not sure this is the way to go," she said. "Perhaps it's best to accept what's happening and fix Simon rather than the phone."

Dilly thought these were wise words, but still wanted to find him, if possible. They shared a milk shake in a fast food chain, sucking up ideas along with the thick creamy milk.

"It could be somebody in the building," said Dilly. "They've hacked into the WiFi and set up the connection. Our winning numbers aren't secret."

"You wouldn't have to hack into it," said Laura, "you could just set it up normally."

"But what it does isn't normal, is it?"

What the connection did certainly was not normal by any stretch of the imagination. You could set up a ridiculously long WiFi name but you couldn't make it do what this one did.

"Unless there's a mad scientist living here," said Dilly.

Laura laughed.

"What's he like?" she asked.

"The mad scientist?"

"No, the boy. Simon."

Dilly's mind changed tack. They'd been so focused on following the lead of the lottery numbers that she'd almost forgotten poor Simon.

"He's thirteen," she said, "and nice." Laura wanted a little more than that. "His family moved into their house a few months ago."

"Like you."

"Like me. His dad's a bit strange. He fought in the war and has a bad temper. He does crosswords and sits a lot. His mum's all over them. I mean she does nothing else but cook and clean and shop and hug them. I'm not sure Simon likes it but he's all locked up." Laura waited for more. "In himself, not in prison. He's clever. He has loads of books in his room and he's interested in everything."

"But?"

"But he's like a flower that can't grow because he's being bullied and it's horrible. It wouldn't happen today."

"Oh yes it would," said Laura. "Boys will be boys. Girls will be girls, too. They bully, too, you know. And adults do it, too. There have always been horrid people around. Mums and dads talk about a golden age but it never was. Every age has its good and bad people. It's how you deal with them."

Dilly knew that this was true but once again couldn't help but be impressed with Laura's insights and wisdom. She really was special. Dilly had seen and heard enough already to know that bullying was ancient and current.

"If I go back there, what should I tell him to do?" Dilly asked.

"You can't tell him to do anything," Laura answered. "He has to work that out for himself."

"So why am I there?" asked Dilly. They'd talked about this before. There was no simple answer then and there was no simple answer now. "Should I tell him to hit them?" she asked. "There's a whole gang. One leader, but a gang."

"You shouldn't tell him what to do at all," said Laura again. "He has to work that out. It might be enough if you're there as a friend. Sounds like he needs one."

"He does," said Dilly. "There are lots of children living there. It's new, like where we live, but it feels different, like it was built for different reasons. He shouldn't be alone. He's really nice and he should have friends."

"You're nice and you should have friends," said Laura. "Things take time."

As ever, Laura sounded wise beyond her years.

"I don't like the idea of him being alone there with those... thugs... around."

"He knows that. It might make a difference. Having a friend on your side is important."

Quite a few pupils at Dilly's new school visited the fast

food place, and one or two recognised her as 'the girl who fainted' but for whatever reason, didn't come over.

"Maybe they're afraid of catching faints," said Dilly, and Laura laughed again.

"You're funny," she said. "Maybe if I wasn't here they'd talk more. They all think I'm a bit weird."

This was true, but Dilly didn't mind. She liked Laura's weirdness and was grateful for her help. Dilly knew that she was putting out strange vibes. Who wouldn't with such a peculiar thing happening in their lives? She had to solve this problem. If she could solve it, all would be well, or if not all, then regret would haunt her and Simon for the rest of their lives.

As if to prove them wrong about their reputations, three girls hesitantly came over to them.

"Are you plotting? You look like you're plotting."

At first, Dilly thought they were being serious, but immediately realised that they were joking. She shook her head.

"You're the fainter, aren't you."

It wasn't so much a question, more an observation.

"She's alright now, though," said Laura.

"I'm Becky," said one of the girls.

"I'm Beth," said the other.

"I'm Miriam," said the third.

"You'd Beth and I were twins with names like that," said Becky, "but we're not."

Dilly and Laura gave their names. Dilly was not sure what to make of this unexpected introduction but Laura seemed quite calm about it. Becky, Beth and Miriam sat themselves down without waiting for an invitation.

"Were you plotting? It looked like you were," said Beth again.

"No," Dilly replied, "what would we plot against?"

"Oh, everything," said Becky. "I bet you have a secret,

though."

Dilly glanced at Laura who kept a poker face.

"It doesn't matter," said Beth. "Take not notice of Becky. She's nosey. You don't have to tell us."

"Although we would like to know," said Becky.

"Becky!" exclaimed Beth, "you're incorrigible," which was a word she'd recently discovered and wanted to use.

The three girls seemed as unusual as Dilly and Laura might have appeared to them. They bounced off each other lightly, truly like triplets, and appeared genuinely interested.

"No plot," said Dilly.

"All the girls talk about you," said Becky.

"Becky!" said Beth, reprimanding her. "Really!"

"It's true," said Becky, "but in a nice way. They wonder if you're alright."

"You mean in the head?" asked Dilly.

"No, just alright. I said it was because you were new and nervous. It must be hard to change schools and not know anyone."

"It was," said Dilly. "It is."

"Well, we're here," said Beth. "We're nice."

"Very nice," said Becky. "And if you are plotting something, please let us plot with you."

Dilly didn't know if Becky was joking or serious. Miriam, meanwhile, sat and listened. She seemed quite shy and in awe of the two noisier girls.

"Take no notice," said Beth. "Secrets are secrets. If you told us, it wouldn't be secret any more, would it. As long as you're alright."

"I'm alright," said Dilly.

"Only you do look a bit... peaky," said Beth.

"Do I?"

"A bit. You're under strain, I can tell."

Dilly smiled. They were funny, these three, and meant

well. They would be nice friends, if she could get over the hump of all that was happening. The whole thing was holding her back, she could feel it. She wanted to move on, to become part of the school, to make new friends and be happy again. How could she when Simon was calling out to her, as she felt he was, even if he did not know it himself. Something was connecting them through time. It was as clear as anything this opaque could be. Unless she sorted it out, found out how and why it was happening and bring it to an end, she would never be at peace here, not at home, not at school, nowhere.

"You're not going to faint again, are you?" said Becky.

Dilly shook her head and said she was fine, just thinking.

"Are they really talking about me?" she asked. "I wish they wouldn't."

"Not so much any more," said Beth. "They did at the time. But they were worried. It was... upsetting. I'll tell them you're okay. You are okay, aren't you?" She said she was. "You can both come round to my house some time, if you like."

"Or mine," said Becky, "although Beth's is nicer."

"Becky's is one of the new towers," said Beth. "Like living in a greenhouse."

"Me too," said Dilly.

"Oops," said Beth, "sorry."

"I'm getting used to it," said Dilly.

They spoke for a while, although Miriam and Laura said surprisingly little. Laura was comfortable with Dilly but not so much with others. She didn't seem uncomfortable, just not as ready to talk.

Once the girls had gone, Dilly asked her, "Didn't you like them?"

"I did, a lot."

"But you didn't say much."

"You'll be their friend, not me."

This was a mysterious thing to say and Dilly would have asked her about it except that something caught her eye.

Outside the fast food shop was a small, bright red van. Etched on one side was the name of the company that had installed their WiFi – AURAL Communications. Dilly hurried Laura outside, dropping half eaten bags of French fries and an empty burger case into the bin. The driver's seat was empty.

"Drat," said Dilly.

"He might not be the same man, anyway," Laura said, holding back for some reason.

"But he might know who did it. We have to ask, Laura. I'm running out of ideas."

They waited five minutes, then ten, but no driver.

"We could take the registration number," said Dilly, "that's what they do on television programmes."

"That won't help us," said Laura, staring at the number plate. "He hasn't done anything wrong. He's probably doing a job. He might be ages."

Dilly did not want to give up. They waited another five minutes, fidgeting and looking highly suspicious. It was no surprise that a community officer approached them and asked what they were doing. As with school and home, the truth was impossible to tell, at least in full.

"We want to speak to the driver," said Dilly.

"Any reason?"

"It's hard to explain. A technical question."

"There are better ways to ask technical questions," said the community officer. "You can call them or chat or email. Customers don't usually hang around on street corners waiting to kidnap the drivers."

"Oh, we're not going to kidnap him," explained Dilly, innocently.

The officer laughed.

"I'm quite good with this kind of thing. What's the problem?"

"It really is hard to explain," said Dilly, panicking.

"Try," said the officer.

Laura came to the rescue.

"Dilly's just moved here. They put in a new WiFi but it's very slow. That's all."

The officer looked sceptical.

"That's a bit vague," she said, "but I honestly don't think the engineer will be able to sort it out on the pavement. That really is not the way to do it. Are you sure you're okay? Is there anything else worrying you?" Any more white lies and the two of them would be in hot water so they shook their heads. "If it is just slow speeds, unplug the modem, wait a minute, then plug it back in again. That's what they'll tell you to do after you wait half an hour on the phone. Have you tried that?" They said they hadn't. "Give it a whirl. Do you know what 'modem' means?"

"'Modulator demodulator'," said Laura, instantly.

The community officer and Dilly looked at her, astonished.

"Impressive," said the officer. I would have been an engineer myself if I were cleverer," she added. "Besides, I like uniforms. Where do you live?" Dilly pointed to the massive building works with towers pointing to the sky like accusing fingers. "Lucky you," said the officer. "Best make your way home and give these people a call," she said nodding at the van. "Chances are that this chap is not the one who did the work for you anyway. Last chance, are you sure you're alright? Nothing secret to tell me? I'm very trustworthy."

They were also relieved that they it didn't look as though they were going to be arrested but for a moment, Dilly thought she could spill the beans and tell the community officer everything, but she didn't. She couldn't.

She might as well tell her that aliens had landed in a flying saucer and asked to take them to their leader. It would be more believable.

"We're fine," said Laura. "Thank you."

"I'll walk you home if you like?"

The officer, like all conscientious community officers, was aware and concerned about all the bad things that happened in the world and was switched on to suspicious situations. This was one. However, she didn't believe the two girls were about to rob a bank, and they didn't look afraid, just uncomfortable. A lot of people became uncomfortable in the presence of uniforms. She did, too. It was easier to wear one than face up to one, even a community officer's. She watched them go, wondering whether to follow but decided against it. A few seconds later, as luck would have it, the driver returned. The officer watched him in case his face was familiar or it turned up on a wanted poster in the sheriff's office. She thought of calling the girls back but what she had told them was true. The chances of him being the one they were looking for were slim, and even if he was, accosting him on the streets was not the way to answer Frequently Asked Questions. She watched him drive away and walked on, thinking about the modem she used as a girl, so many years ago, which was painfully slow and totally unreliable. She wished she'd studied harder and become an engineer after all. So engrossed was she in her thoughts of different paths taken in life that she forgot the main rule in such situations of possible suspicious circumstances – write down the registration number. Had she done so, she would have been surprised because it had changed from the one the girls had seen. It was now a non-standard combination of letters and numbers, unusual for company cars and vans. It read simply: YPH1.

0000 1011: NORMAN FELL

Norman was a waste of space. His father told him, his mother told him and his two elder brothers told him, too. Fortunately for him but unfortunately for everyone else, he didn't believe it. In fact, he believed the opposite, that his space was the most important of all. He proved this to himself by bullying everyone that entered his space, and often even if they didn't. That was rare because according to Norman, his space was everywhere. It moved with him. When he was at school, it was there. When he was in the playground, it was there. When he and his gang walked the estate, it was there. He owned it all.

His gang knew this and didn't argue the point. By being with him, they owned the estate, too, and the roads, the flats, the playground, everything. That made them powerful. Norman knew this and kept them in check. If any of them got uppity and challenged them, he'd take them by the scruff of the neck, look them in the eyes and let them know who was in charge, who was boss. He didn't have to do it often. He'd done it once to the biggest boy, smaller than him, and that was enough.

'Norman' wasn't a scary name. There were Normans on TV and cinema who were charming, funny and harmless Normans, but this particular one had no charm, no humour but plenty of threat. As tall as he was, his brothers were taller and continued to call him a waste of space up to the age of fourteen, by which time they had left school and gone off to make trouble in the world. Fourteen years of name calling left its mark. You could almost see the mark in his vicious, angry eyes and his flaming red hair. Red hair was quite rare and Norman considered that a sign of his importance. At fourteen, he felt he could bully the world. He'd never met anyone who could stand up to him and he hated all of them. No, he did not hate them, he simply felt nothing for them. They were weak whilst he was strong. They were goody goodies whilst he was a bandit, a rebel, a law unto himself.

When he saw the coronation of the queen, he saw himself crowned, in his mind's eye. Why not? Strong people should rule and he was strong. What good was a girl doing being queen? Norman's dad had fought in the war. He was tough. A tough guy. He didn't stand fools gladly. That's what this country needed, a strong leader, not – a girl!

He proved his strength by making as many children as possible fear him. He pinched, he punched, he slapped, he bit, he spat, he poked, he picked, he tore into others with controlled venom, knowing they were scared of him. He hardly knew their names, none of them. They weren't children, they were weaklings, there to let him frighten them, to show them who was boss. He made them give him money if it looked like they had any. He never planned his bullying. He wasn't especially bright and wouldn't have been able to plan much if he tried. He went about his business and shoved out the way anyone who stood in his. Sometimes, they weren't in his way at all, but he took a dislike to them anyway and hurt them. Not so much that he would get into trouble, but enough to frighten them and stop them from telling their mummies and daddies or their stupid teachers. He disliked his teachers most of all. Norman couldn't stand being told what to do. He knew what he wanted to do and did it. So far in his short life, he'd learned not a single thing from a single teacher. He bunked off school whenever he felt like it and the teachers didn't follow it up because they were glad to be rid of him. Lessons bored him. The only lessons he liked were woodwork and metalwork because tools were like weapons. When he held them, he felt more like a king than ever. He was no good at either, that goes without saying. His wood joints wobbled and his metal ones creaked. But Norman couldn't care less. School was a pain and he couldn't wait to get out into the proper world where he could prove to his rotten family that he wasn't a waste of space at all.

Meanwhile, in assembly, he would torment whoever looked ready to be tormented. This morning it was the clever clogs whose name he could never remember. He poked him in the back and pinched his backside.

"Mummy's boy," he whispered, "give us sixpence. Go on, no one's looking."

Indeed, no one was looking. Everyone was listening to the headteacher who telling a story about angels at a meal with giant spoons, so long that the angels could not feed themselves. The only solution was to feed each other. The headteacher was telling the school about generosity and kindness as Norman Fell bullied the boy in front of him, extorting money. Simon tried to take no notice. He shifted in his seat and wondered what would happen if he stood up and shouted that he was being robbed, that the boy behind him was cruel, vicious and mean. Would they take him seriously and act or would they tell him to sit down and be quiet? And even if they took him seriously, what would they do? Would the headteacher cane Norman? Surely that would make matters worse. Norman would certainly come after Simon in a big way, a frightening way.

He turned around, fighting back tears, whispering, "Leave me alone!"

"Or what?" Norman replied.

"Shh!" A teacher hearing the whispering. "No talking."

The teachers weren't fools, of course. They knew that Norman Fell was a bad egg. They didn't think of him as 'difficult', he was simply 'bad'. But even they didn't know how bad, and what he was doing to many other boys. There were no channels of discussion open. Unless he was caught red handed, or someone would report him with clear evidence, he remained a 'bad' boy and the teachers had no power to make him a 'good' boy. They themselves had forgotten what it was to be a child and how it felt to be fearful and powerless in the face of bigger bullies.

"Make it a shilling," whispered Norman. "Now. Else two bob after school."

Simon would not give him the money. Something inside told him that it would not be the end of the bullying. He might give sixpence now but he would have to give a shilling tomorrow. And if he gave a shilling 'after school', they all knew what after school meant. No teachers, no rules, no adults, just him against Norman and his gang and another beating, whether or not he gave Norman a shilling.

The school sang 'All things bright and beautiful' which Simon tried to sing with hot tears stinging his eyes. He could see no beauty nor any brightness, just this monster patiently waiting to pounce.

He remembered the Dilly ghost and wished she were here now to witness this, to give him support and somehow scare Norman. But she was not here. He had not seen her for weeks and wondered if she would ever pop into his world again.

The day passed slowly and he could not concentrate on his lessons. He saw Norman now and again but the bully did not even glance at him. Simon sensed that he saw him, though, and was pretty sure that Noman knew he was scared to death. Simon's fear fed the beast.

When the bell went for the end of day, Simon packed up his books slowly. Maybe he was wrong. Maybe Norman had forgotten and moved on to other victims. Was it wrong to hope so? Was it cowardice to hope that the bully would pick on someone else and leave him alone? It probably was, but Simon already considered himself a coward. He didn't want that, though. He didn't want anyone else to suffer. He wanted instead all the bullying to stop, that God would have heard the headmaster's story and the school hymns and showed His kindness by striking Norman Fell dead with a bolt of lightning. How about that? Was that wrong, too? Possibly, but Simon didn't care. Just end this.

He walked slowly. If he'd known another way home, he would have taken it, but he didn't. There probably wasn't one. The people who had designed the estate placed the school right in the middle so that most of the pupils could walk there and walk home safely. It was what that called a 'progressive' school with lots of new fangled ideas. They tried to change everything and build a better future, but they could not change human nature. They could not stop children being upset, hurt and put upon. They tried, at least some of them tried, but they could not put right what they did not see. In the end, you had to fight your own battles, which was a lesson that some children knew from the day they were born, and some never could until the day they died, which was a terrible waste. Some learned it but could not put it into practise. David learned it against Goliath, apparently, and although Simon knew the story, he didn't fully believe it. Maybe Goliath was not so big or David not so small. Maybe David got lucky or Goliath wasn't so brave. Maybe David cheated. Simon had had the bible thumped into him for years, but he was an imaginative boy with a mind of his own and he already doubted so much of what he'd learned.

He got home without a scratch. Norman and his gang either failed to find him or, more likely, had completely forgotten about him. How could they forget, Simon thought as he tumbled onto his bed. He would remember forever the pokes and pinches and the helplessness. He would know forever that boys like Norman could get away with threats and hurts in front of adults who, for all their wisdom, did not see what was right under their noses. Simon was terrified yet Norman Fell had in all likelihood forgotten about him completely. That's how Norman operated, through fear.

"Are you alright, Simon?" his mother asked, looking in furtively. She was still afraid of seeing the ghost again. Nothing could persuade her otherwise. Nothing, on the other hand, could persuade Simon's father, that the ghost had been real. Real or not, Simon's mother was convinced the house was haunted and prayed every night that the ghost would go and haunt someone else's house.

"I'm alright mum. Going to do some homework."

"You look white as a sheet," said his mother, coming over and feeling his forehead. "Well, you're not hot. You don't seem to be ill. You haven't seen... the..."

"There's nothing to see, mum," he insisted.

His mother looked around the room which would never be the same again. For a while it had been a normal boy's bedroom, but now it was the lair of a spectral girl that only she could see. She was sure it was this spectre that was frightening her son. The thought that he was afraid of anything else didn't occur to her. She'd told her husband but he had no patience for silly ghost stories. He had no idea what his wife had seen, but as she hadn't seen it since, he left it at that. If she saw the wretched thing again, he would take her to a doctor.

"If you're sure, then," said Simon's mother with one more look around. "Dinner in half hour. Wash your hands and face first. You can say grace tonight, Daddy said so."

She left him alone, agitated and angry for reasons she did not understand.

"Grace!" muttered Simon. "Fat lot of good that does."

"You're in a bad mood, aren't you?"

He'd heard nothing, but there she was, the Dilly ghost, hiding in the corner.

"My mum! If she sees you, she'll have a fit! You just missed her."

Dilly took a deep breath. She'd been sitting in a geography lesson of all things when her phone buzzed. The school did not generally allow phones in school, but because Dilly had had her episode, they let her keep it for a while, for security. Little did they know it was the very thing that troubled her. It buzzed and showed the flashing WiFi connection. Here, in school, once again where it should not and could not have been. She didn't hesitate. She knew instinctively that Simon was in trouble and she'd tapped it. If she fainted in the geography lesson, so be it. Simon came first.

"That was a scare," said Dilly. "Are you alright? You don't look it."

Simon shrugged. He was ashamed of his fear.

"How come you're here?" he asked, rather abruptly. "I didn't think I'd see you again."

"I didn't think I'd come here again," said Dilly, "not after scaring your mum half to death. Sorry about that. Is she alright?"

"Not really," said Simon. "She still thinks she's seen a ghost, and she has, hasn't she?"

"Only to you," said Dilly. "I'm really not, but you'll never believer me. You seem alright. I was worried. I thought..."

She hesitated and Simon asked, "What did you think?"

"That you were in trouble."

Simon looked down. He could hardly face the Dilly ghost. Even though she wasn't real, he was ashamed still of his weakness.

"I'm alright," he said.

"Well you don't look it," said Dilly, "and I don't think

I would be here if everything was hunky dory."

"Everything was what?"

"Hunky dory," Dilly repeated, as if that would explain the meaning. "Fine. Fine and dandy. Is it them again?" she asked.

Simon was impressed. Neither his parents nor his teachers had cottoned on to what was truly going on, but this half visible girl seemed to know immediately, and she was concerned.

"I thought they were going to get me on the way home tonight," he said. "Norman said he would but he didn't."

"Norman?"

"The leader. I hate him."

Dilly made her way further into Simon's room, looking again at all his books, his science gadgets, his tidy cub board and grown up wallpaper. He was much cleverer than boys she knew, though she didn't know that many. But he seemed even more glum than the last visit, and he'd been fairly glum then. She wasn't. Oddly, Dilly was feeling rather pleased with herself. She'd made the leap from then to now, or perhaps from now to then, without hesitation, in the middle of a geography lesson. She hadn't been afraid and she wasn't afraid now. She knew that familiarity bred contempt so she was trying hard not to be too familiar with Simon's world, nevertheless, she felt as if she was mastering this so far inexplicable bridge-across-the-ages.

"What are you going to do about it, then?"

Simon had no answer so Dilly, not wanting to lecture him, and anyway not sure of what she should say, changed the subject.

"This is new," she said, pointing at a long, narrow and shallow blue tin sitting on the table.

"Mum bought it for me," said Simon. "It's a paint box."

"Open it," said Dilly.

Inside were about twenty small dips filled with coloured

paints. Laying next to them was a brush, a painting book and a glass jar filled with water.

"Oh, it's beautiful," said Dilly. "Have you painted anything yet?"

He hadn't. He wanted to but he was so restless, he couldn't concentrate.

"I probably won't be very good at it."

"Oh, silly, you know that's not true. You could paint me. How about that?"

"Would you let me?" Simon asked.

"As long as you don't show it to your mum. She'll have a fit."

Simon laughed, that lovely light laugh she'd heard before. He thought about it a moment then filled the glass jar with water and opened the book which was full of empty white pages and sat down.

"You'll have to keep still," he told her.

Dilly stood as still as she could, even though she continued to tremble like a proper ghost. Simon dipped the brush into the jar, then began mixing the paints.

"Don't you want to draw me first?" Dilly asked.

"No, too easy," said Simon. "That would be like painting by numbers."

"Only my art teacher said…"

"Shush!" He instructed her. "I can't concentrate if you chat."

Dilly shushed, not upset or offended but more impressed. She watched Simon paint silently and attentively, looking from her to his canvas, studying the paints and the mixes he was making.

"You look like a proper artist," said Dilly.

She wanted to ask him more questions and nose around his room a bit more, but he was so engrossed in the painting that she decided not to disturb him and be told off again. How strange, she thought, to see a boy's room, or any

room, without a computer. She would have asked him how
he survived, but they all did. There was not a single
computer in a single home in a single country anywhere on
the planet. How different that was, she realised. How
different everything was because of it. She couldn't
imagine any of her old friends or new ones sitting down
painting each other like this. It was something she would
ask Laura to do when she got back.

Back.

For a moment she felt giddy and had to steady herself.
Simon asked her if she was alright. Just thinking of Laura
and 'back' had made her feel dizzy, as if looking down
from a great height. What if she could not return? What if
she'd become over confident and ought not to have come?
But no, she could not believe it was wrong. She had to have
faith in whatever was happening that it meant her no harm,
that in fact it meant her only good. And the same for Simon.

"You're moving," he said.

She composed herself. Simon looked so grown up. All
he needed was a beret, a smock and a palette on his arm and
he'd be a young Picasso. How could she make him happy,
this talented boy who was being persecuted to death by a
fool who would not know what to do with a paintbrush
other than poke someone in the eye with it. Again she asked
herself if she could do anything directly, but she couldn't.
She was only half in this time, not even half, probably. She
couldn't touch anything, couldn't feel anything, couldn't
taste anything. And only Simon could see her, in the right
light, apart from his mother who seemed far more sensitive
than others. No, there was nothing she could do directly,
although she would like to do the paintbrush poking on this
Fell boy, oh how she would.

"What are you thinking about?" Simon asked.

"I thought I wasn't allowed to talk." Simon apologised
and said he was nearly finished. "I was thinking about why

I'm here," Dilly went on. "I'm sure it's to help you, but I don't know how."

"You are helping me," Simon replied, pausing for a moment. "It's much better when you're here."

Dilly smiled.

"Am I allowed to smile?"

Simon blushed then carried on painting. Dilly thought, what a fantastic thing to say, that things were much better when she was there. Would they be much worse when she left? They seemed to have become friends so here was yet another friend that would come and go. She'd seen Beth, Becky and Miriam a few times and they were getting on. As for Laura with her far away look and even further away talk, what would become of their friendship?

"I'm done," said Simon.

Dilly cut short her reflections and took a look at Simon's first painting.

"Oh, wow, Simon, that's... that's unbelievable!"

"Unbelievable good or bad?"

"Good of course, silly. More than good. It's fabulous!"

Simon was chuffed. He knew he could get Dilly's likeness, but the painting was more than that. It captured her spirit, or better, it captured the idea that she was a spirit.

"Not too ghostly?" he asked.

"Just the right amount," said Dilly. "I wish I could take it with me," she said, trying to touch the paper and seeing her hand go through it, like a proper ghost.

"I'll save it for you," said Simon, "although..."

"Although you might not be able to save it for ever," said Dilly. "That's okay. At least I've seen it now and I can keep it in my memory forever. And I know how clever you are. Gosh, Simon, I look really nice!"

They laughed because she wasn't showing off, it was truly a delightful painting. Dilly asked him if he was set on being a scientist. Wouldn't he rather be a famous artist like

Picasso or… she tried to name more but didn't know any. She could not take her eyes off the painting. She was so captivated that she did not hear the footsteps outside. Nor did Simon. The door opened as Simon's mother came to remind him that it was time to eat. She did not manage a single word, though. The only thing that Simon and Dilly heard was an almighty scream followed by a thud as Simon's mother fainted in a heap.

Simon turned to his spectral friend in despair but the Dilly ghost was gone.

0000 1100: FUNK

"So remember, everyone, the warm front is curved, the cold front is sharp and the occluded…"

"Sir!" A voice called from the back of the class. "Dilly's in a funk again."

The geography teacher immediately forgot about occluded fronts and hurried over to Dilly's desk. She was sitting upright, holding her phone, staring straight ahead but seeing nothing.

"Dilly?"

Laura, sitting next to her friend, immediately cottoned on to what was happening. The last thing Dilly would want would be another hospital visit, so she said,

"It's alright, sir. Just a second."

She whispered something in Dilly's ear and immediately Dilly blinked and pulled herself together.

"Sorry," she said, as if nothing had happened, "daydreaming."

Yet it was obvious something had happened. She looked shocked and shaky.

The geography teacher, as obsessed as he was with occluded fronts, sensed that this was more than daydreaming. He asked Laura to take Dilly to Miss Roberts, let her decide. The other pupils watched as the two girls left, some of them whispering, all of them slightly uncomfortable. Dilly was becoming quite popular and they were beginning to forget the first day fainting fit, but this brought it back. It didn't look like an illness, it was disturbing. Very few people like 'different' and Dilly was certainly different.

Miss Roberts sat her down in the office and said she was

going to call Dilly's mother.

"No, no, miss, please don't. I'm fine. Mum's busy and she'll only be worried."

"Is there something to worry about, Dilly? I know that the hospital have given you all clear otherwise I'd contact them again right now. I'm afraid I will have to tell your mother, though. It wouldn't be right for me not to tell her."

She gave Dilly a glass of water and allowed Laura to stay, asking gently for an explanation. Dilly stuck to the daydreaming story and Laura backed her up. Miss Roberts did not want to push too hard and put Dilly under stress. Nevertheless, she insisted that she would have to tell Dilly's mother. Laura took Dilly's hand and told her not to worry. It would be fine. Dilly was not convinced. She didn't want her mother distracted from her work, worrying about nothing. Well, it was something, but nobody could help. This was between her, Simon and the mystery that linked them.

Miss Roberts tried to ease the tension by asking whether the picture she'd given them was any use for their project?

"Project?" Dilly asked without thinking. "Oh, yes, very useful."

"Which teacher is it for?" Miss Roberts asked.

"It's just for ourselves," Laura interrupted. "Dilly wants to know more about her new home. Me too."

"Well, that's unusual," said Miss Roberts, "but good for you. I must say, it was a decent painting. Grandfather had hidden talents."

The words made Dilly recall what she'd said to Simon, just before… she took a deep breath, trying to hold back the shock of what had happened, not to give anything away. Her mind was full of fast receding memories – of Simon's unhappiness, of his portrait and of his screaming mother. She also heard Laura's words that came at the same time, 'Dilly, it's me, Laura. Time to come home.' Those were the words Laura had whispered in the geography class, just after Simon's mother had seen her. The scream might have sent her back home anyway but Laura's kind words brought her back in a gentler fashion. Nevertheless, Dilly was still edgy. Would she ever return to Simon again? She wanted so much to help him but if his mother saw her a third time, heaven knew what would happen.

Dilly would have loved to tell Miss Roberts everything, but she daren't. As kind and understanding as the teacher was, she would never accept this story. Dilly would end up in hospital again with doctors poking around inside her head. Once more, she wondered if perhaps there was something actually to find if they did poke around. As real as it seemed to her, could it all be an illusion, the result of a real problem?

"Dilly?"

"Yes miss, sorry."

"You really do disappear, don't you?" Dilly blushed and said she was trying not to. Miss Roberts laughed and said, "You must be getting used to your new home by now, and us, here in DoTheGirls School."

"DoTheBoys School," said Dilly with only a slight pause. "Nicholas Nickleby, Charles Dickens."

"Crikey, Dilly, you are a star. You've read it?" She had. "There's hope yet," said Miss Roberts. "Now, what am I going to do with you – and you, Laura. You always seem to be on hand to help Dilly, don't you?"

"She's my friend, miss. She's got other friends, too, now, but I was first."

"Yes you were, weren't you. And you haven't been here that long either, have you?" She hadn't. Just those few months. "You have other friends?" Miss Roberts asked Dilly.

"Beth and Becky. Miriam in the reading group. Rahima in…"

"No, no, you don't need to list them," said Miss Roberts. "As long as you are settling in. Sometimes moves don't work and schools don't fit. It happens. I was concerned that maybe you were unhappy here."

"I was miss," said Dilly, honestly, "but I think I'll be alright."

"And home?"

"That will be alright, too," she answered.

She meant it. One thing she'd learned from glimpses of the past was that everything wasn't always golden in the golden ages of memory. There was unhappiness then just as there was now. People could be cruel as well as kind. The architects who designed houses now might be going through a peculiar phase, or drunk when they sat at their drawing boards, but when this place was finished, it might be just as nice as it once was, in a different way.

Miss Roberts let them go. School had ended anyway so they went back to Dilly's house for tea. When they arrived, Dilly's mother embraced her daughter as if they'd been apart for a century.

"Darling, what happened? What happened? Come in and tell me. Laura, sweetie, come in, too."

Obviously, Miss Roberts had been true to her word and called Dilly's mother.

"Nothing happened, mum," said Dilly. "I flipped out for a moment, day dreaming, that's all."

"Flipped out?" her mother repeated. "What does that mean?"

Laura tried to help.

"It was only a moment," she said. "She didn't faint or anything."

Dilly's mother squeezed Dilly's hand, not convinced.

"I'm tempted to call the doctor. She said…"

"No, mum, you mustn't. I'm fine. Look at me! There's nothing wrong."

It didn't matter how much Dilly protested, her mother was not persuaded. Dilly was her beautiful daughter, dragged into this new life kicking and screaming. If she was unhappy, her mother would do anything to help, even bite the bullet and move back. She asked Laura to confirm and Laura reassured her.

"It was just a few seconds, Mrs Paget," said Laura. "I think Dully has a heightened imagination."

Dilly's mother laughed and said, "Such a fancy phrase for a young girl, Laura. You know, we've never met your parents, have we? They should come round some time. I don't think Dilly has even been to your house, have you, love?"

She hadn't. This was something of a puzzle as Laura had been to Dilly's house quite a few times. Both Dilly and her mother knew better than to push. There were often reasons for non invitations, and meanness didn't seem at all like a Laura family trait.

"I'll ask," said Laura. "They're very busy, though. They travel a lot."

"But they don't leave you alone, surely?" Dilly's mother asked.

"Oh no, never, of course not. I'll ask. Promise."

Dilly's mother left them to prepare a tea, anxious now not only about her own daughter, but her daughter's strange friend. She had hoped to start this new life free of troubles and worries, but here they were again. Clearly, money wasn't the only source of anxiety in the world.

While she was out, Laura said, "Dilly? Are you truly alright? What happened?"

This was the first chance Dilly had had to tell Laura about the latest disaster. That's what it felt like, a catalogue of disasters with no meaning and no end result. Would they go on forever? She told Laura who listened attentively.

"That's good," she whispered when Dilly had finished.

"Good? How is it good?" Dilly asked.

"Oh," said Laura, "the painting, that's beautiful, don't you think? If he can do something like that, he can do anything."

"He can't paint Norman Fell out of his life, can he?" Dilly said.

"Maybe he can," replied Laura, "in a way. He has to. Sounds like a troubled person."

Once more, Dilly registered Laura's extreme empathy.

"And his mother saw me again!" Dilly said. "How's he going to explain that?"

"You have to believe that everything happens for a reason," said Laura, sounding like the wisest head in the land. "It might not make sense now, but it will."

Dilly was more fond of Laura than any of her new friends, but she could be astonishingly adult, more adult than even adults ought to be. This made her smile and she held her hand.

"I don't know what I'd do if you weren't here," said Dilly. "I'd have to keep all this in my head alone. I couldn't do it."

Dilly's mother could hardly sleep that night. She tossed and turned, trying to work out what was going on. Nothing she came up with seemed close to the truth. The hospital had been as sure as they could be that nothing was physically wrong or even different with Dilly. They'd done scans and investigations and taken enough pictures to fill the National Gallery but all seemed well. This was a relief, of course, but Dilly was going through some kind of difficult phase. Mrs Paget tried to remember what it was like being thirteen, close to fourteen, but she couldn't. It was impossible to relive that age again, even in recollections. Certainly, she never fainted or went into funks during geography lessons. And why was Dilly so obsessed with the past? Not many children were. Perhaps it was because this whole building site where they lived now was so new? Did the ghost of what it once was haunt it? Maybe Dilly felt disconnected. Even so, to have these episodes, perhaps others that Mrs Paget knew nothing about, that was worrying.

Dilly was beloved more than she could know. When she grew up, when she had a child of her own, she would know then what it was like to love a child and to worry about them. She felt guilty that they'd moved, all because she'd wanted a new and better life. How frustrating was that, to try and do the right thing and end up finding out that you'd done the wrong thing. And as for her Art, what value was that if Dilly was unhappy? She could paint and craft wonderful things until the end of time, but if her daughter was miserable and ill, she would rather burn it all to ashes.

The next day she called Miss Roberts.

"It was a blip," said Miss Roberts, talking of Dilly's episode in the geography lesson. "We're all keeping an eye on her. If it happens again, or something similar, then maybe call the hospital again, but she seems fine, generally."

"You don't think she's unhappy?"

"Not as much. Something's troubling her, but heaven knows what it is. She won't talk to me."

"Or me," said Dilly's mother. "It's a worry. Do you know Laura's family? I know you can't say much, but are they okay? Is Laura a good friend?"

"I think she is," said Miss Roberts. "I haven't met them but one or other teacher must have done. They have a reputation, you know." Dilly's mother asked wheat kind of reputation. "For being very clever. Cleverer than most of the teachers put together," Miss Roberts laughed, "but kind. Good people."

"Only we haven't seen them, and Dilly has never been to their house."

"I wouldn't worry about that," said Miss Roberts. "They haven't been here that long either and I know they are busy. Laura is a special girl, very affectionate, very bright. She doesn't have too many friends, in fact until Dilly came along, she didn't have any. A loner."

Dilly's mother wasn't concerned about 'loners'. She was never one herself, but she didn't have the suspicions that others had of the word. Besides, she'd met Laura a free times and liked her, despite the mysteries surrounding her.

"Do you think..." Dilly's mother started, then hesitated. Miss Roberts prompted her onwards. "Do your think we should move back?"

Miss Roberts did not hesitate.

"No, I don't think that's a good idea at all. Honestly, I think Dilly will settle in. She's already met other girls her age and seems to be settling. If you move back, she might be plagued by a sense of guilt or failure, and whatever it is that's bothering her wouldn't disappear. Have you thought of taking her to a counsellor?"

Dilly's mother had thought of it, but Dilly was adamant, she would not and could not speak to a stranger.

Coincidentally, Dilly was saying the same thing at the same moment to Laura.

"There's nothing wrong with me, is there?"

"Nothing," said Laura. "What's happening is real."

"But I can't tell them, can I?" Laura agreed, she couldn't. "So what can I do?"

"You're doing it already," said Laura.

Dilly was puzzled by her new friend. She loved the way Laura supported her. There was nobody on Earth who would see things the way Laura did and offer belief the way she did. It was unique. But there was a puzzle about her that Dilly couldn't solve. She wanted to ask but she didn't know how to ask, or even what to ask. She was scared, too, of upsetting her. She couldn't bear to lose Laura. She'd would feel so alone, unbearably alone, even with some of her new friends hovering around. Miriam was a bright and funny girl who was as down to Earth as Earth would allow, while Beth and Becky seemed joined at the waist, both fond of 'the new girl'. But none of them knew what Laura knew so none of them could offer what Dilly needed.

"How am I doing it already?" Dilly asked.

"By being you," said Laura, "kind and brave and caring. That's all he needs."

There it was again, that hint of Laura knowing more than she should. But it didn't matter. It was what Dilly needed more than anything else. In a way she could not understand yet, it was what everybody needed at least once in their lives but often never knew it, absolute belief and faith from another person.

The Dilly ghost had come and gone two weeks ago. It was enough time for Simon's mother to insist that they ask the council to let them move. The council said no.

"But it's haunted," insisted Simon's mother.

His father looked on with a weary expression. He'd asked her to think about it before calling the council but she was insistent.

"Madam," said the council agent, "as you very well know, the houses are new and in great demand. You yourselves waited eighteen months before this one was finished. How can it be haunted when you are the first people to live in it?"

"I don't know," said Simon's mother, "but it is. You wouldn't want to live in a haunted house, would you?"

"I don't believe in such things, and neither should you. If this was an ancient castle with rusting armour and hidden staircases, I might understand, but in your lovely knew home, no. I don't know what it is you saw, but it is not a ghost and is not a good reason for moving home. Besides, we would have nowhere else to put you. Every unit is booked and there's a waiting list."

"I cannot live here scared out of my wits," said Simon's mother.

"I can arrange for someone to come and talk to you, if you like," said the housing agent, a touch impatient. "You can show them the ghost."

"I can't show them the ghost!" Simon's mother exclaimed. "It doesn't hang around waiting to be seen. It pops up when you least expect it."

"I'm sorry," said the agent.

"I can prove it," said Simon's mother. "I have a painting of it."

Silence, then, "A painting?"

"My son did it, when the ghost was here."

Simon's mother held the painting in her hand. It was remarkable, and in a way she was proud that her son could do such a thing at his young age, but it was evidence. Surely, the woman on the phone would acknowledge it.

"That's no proof, I'm afraid.".

"I don't know why you can't believe me," said Simon's mother. "And even if you don't, isn't it enough that I'm scared to death."

"You said to one of my colleagues that the ghost was a girl, about the same age as your son, yes?" That was correct. "Did the child look threatening in any way?"

"No, but it vanished as soon as I screamed."

"Was your son scared?"

"Well, no…"

"He painted the ghost while it was there?"

"Yes, but…"

"I wish I could ease your mind but obviously I don't fully understand what's happening there. I get the feeling though, that whatever it is, it isn't dangerous."

"How can you say that? You've not see it!"

Simon's father intervened.

"Darling," he said, "let's talk about it some more. The lady has been very kind."

He took the big black phone gently from his wife's hand before she had time to slam it down in frustration and calmly told the lady that he would discuss the matter further with his wife. The discussion was awkward because of the painting. Whatever his beliefs about ghosts and spooky goings on, the painting was real. Simon's father was tempted to tear it up but Simon desperately wanted to keep it, and his wife, though scared to look at it, needed it as evidence.

"You don't seriously want to move because of this, do you, my dear?" he asked. "We're so comfortable here. I am, anyway. It's everything we've ever wanted. We'll never get anything as lovely as this again, you know."

"We might," she said, then turning to Simon who had been listening in discomfort to these conversations, "Son, do you want to stay here?"

Simon liked his room and his home. If he wanted to move, it wasn't because of the Dilly ghost, in fact she was the main reason he was keen to stay. If he had to leave at all, it would be because of Norman Fell and his gang, but he could not tell his mother and father this, nor his teacher. The only one he could tell was the Dilly ghost, the very reason his mother had decided to uproot them all and run away.

Run away. The words sounded cowardly to him. Was he really going to let empty headed, cruel bullies get the better of him? He sat on the end of his bed kicking his heels together, making a clacking noise that helped him concentrate. He picked up the painting of the Dilly ghost, grateful that his father hadn't torn it in half or that his mother hadn't confiscated it. Who was this girl he'd painted and who came to him so unexpectedly? Was she like the Virgin Mary or a religious vision he'd read and heard about. She didn't have a halo and she didn't talk like an angel, in fact she seemed more down to Earth than many of the people he knew at the church his mother insisted they attend. She didn't come with messages or answers, or with descriptions of some beautiful place with trees, front lawns, identical families with one one son and one daughter walking their well behaved dog on a sunny day. He'd seen that picture on a booklet pushed through their letterbox and wondered where it was. The Dilly ghost seemed, well, ordinary. The most important thing was that she was there for him, but what could she actually do? She couldn't touch anything, and even if she could, she would hardly be able to take on Norman and his thugs. She was not strong or aggressive or scary in any way. For a ghost, she was totally out of character. Yet she was there and he liked her and even needed her. If only he could work out why she'd popped into his life.

He gave up tapping together and decided to head down to his secret lair near the reservoir. Maybe the Dilly ghost was there like she was before, waiting for him.

She wasn't.

The place was deserted so Simon went for for a walk, counting insects and spotting butterflies. For a desolate place, it was actually quite busy. Perhaps this was rush hour for wild life, gathering food and doing what insects, creepy crawlies, moths, butterflies and birds did best, which was to eat, sleep and multiply, despite humans messing up their homes. Simon tried not to trample too much and to keep on a well trodden path, but the path was not well trodden and he supposed that quite a few bugs had had to avoid his big human feet.

They fascinated him. They were so active, so focused on what they were doing. He doubted that any of the aphids he saw were fearful of bullying aphids, or whether any of the common blues were fearful of common red admirals. He doubted it. If he looked carefully, he saw millions of ants and other bugs scuttling around, all with direction and energy. It was riveting. If only he could be like that, focused and single minded, not scuppered by the thuggish Norman Fells of this world.

He kept stopping, hoping against hope to see the Dilly ghost, but all was quiet. He even called her name, but it felt out of place to make human noises in this natural habitat. Gradually, he calmed down. He had been agitated when he set out, worried that he'd upset his parents who were arguing about moving, upset that he'd done nothing to stop the threats and that no one, apart from the Dilly ghost, was willing to help. No one was even remotely aware of it.

He crouched down and allowed an ant to crawl over his fingers. It tickled, and he laughed. A whole colony of ants were busying themselves around his feet. How many? A thousand? A million? A trillion? And in the whole of this unused space beside the reservoir, how many there? And other creepy crawlies. Countless. And not a single one of them was interested in him, his problems or his family's or any of the human race. They just got on with what they had to do to keep alive and make homes for their baby ants, all one zillion of them. Maybe that's what he should do, forget Norman Fell and the countless times he'd humiliated him, called him every horrible name under the sun, hit him, hurt him, struck him, bashed him, bruised him and made him feel as low as these ants crawling all around his feet.

He stood up and took a deep breath. What would the Dilly ghost say? How could she help him? Was it different for a girl, different even more for a ghost?

His head was full of the many times Norman and his thugs had poked him, pinched him and punched him. Even when they passed him by and ignored him, they seemed to know his fear, know that he was there for the taking, and that was just as bad if not worse. Tears welled in his eyes but he would not cry, not for this, not for them. There would be other things in the future to cry about, probably, and he did not want to waste tears on these wretched boys.

As if the Powers That Be had designed the world especially to punish him, Simon looked up and with a mixture of emotions ranging from outright disbelief to outright dread he saw the lanky figure of Norman Fell ambling towards him.

0000 1110: THE SCENE AT THE CANAL

Norman carried a long package over his shoulder held with one hand, and a bag held in the other. Simon froze. The tall boy came on, not seeing anything but the ground, head down, in a world of his own. When he was a few yards away from Simon he seemed to recognise someone else was there and tilted his head up.

Simon was astonished to see that Norman's eyes were red, almost as red as his uncut, untidy hair. One of them was slightly black and blue around the edges. They stood there facing each other like gunmen ready to draw. Simon could do or say nothing. His mouth was dry and his muscles had suddenly lost all power to obey. He almost toppled over like a statue, but he didn't, he held his ground.

Norman stared at him, his eyes, which were supposed to be windows on the soul, showing nothing. Whatever was going on inside his head was privy to him alone.

"What are you doing here?" Norman asked. There not much interest in the question, and, for a change, no threat. Simon didn't answer. "You fishing?" Simon managed to shake his head. "Only this is my spot, or that is, over there. If you take it, I'll wallop you."

Simon managed to turn towards the spot Norman pointed at.

"I don't go fishing," he whispered.

"I do," said Norman.

Now what made Simon say what he said was a mystery to him then and for the rest of his life, though he never regretted it.

"You've been crying," he said.

Norman scowled and said, "I ain't."

For a moment, Simon felt sympathy for this lanky lout. He'd obviously been hit, maybe by his father or brothers. He was as put down by them as Simon was by him. Nevertheless, Simon could not forget how Norman made him feel and he needed to handle this moment right. In a second it would be gone.

"I'll show you how to fish, if you want," said Norman Fell.

If Norman had come up with a quote from Shakespeare or danced a ballet pas de deux, Simon could not have been more shocked. He didn't answer.

"Suit yourself," said Norman and trudged on.

Simon followed, in a daze, his head a turmoil of clashing thoughts. Should he run, should he stop and call for help, what should he do? He meekly followed, letting whatever was to happen play out.

The wild area where they walked was separated from the reservoir by a metal fence. There was no official way into the reservoir area other than the main gates on the other side, about a mile away. Yet, unless Norman was planning on fishing for ants, he headed on with a purpose. After a few minutes, they came to a thickly scrubbed area into which Norman ducked and Simon followed. They came out moments later almost head on into the wire fence. But it was not intact. At the bottom was hole about a metre in diameter.

"If you tell anyone about this, I'll nobble you," said Norman.

Simon nodded, no longer totally scared but also partly intrigued.

They climbed through and Simon saw that the reservoir itself still lay some distance away. Between it and them was a canal of some sort.

"You can't fish in the reservoir," said Norman. "You know why?" Simon did not know why. "Because there are no fish, stupid.".

The word 'stupid' needled Simon. He was about a hundred times cleverer than the tall, older boy, but for the time being he was in his world and in his power and reduced to 'stupid'.

Norman lay down the rod and opened the bag. Inside were all the supplies needed for a few hours solitary fishing, including a small folding stool.

"You'll have to stand," said Norman.

Simon would have thought the world upside down if Norman had offered him the stool and stood himself.

"I cut the hole about three years ago," Norman said, proudly. "I left a bit like a hinge to close it. They've never found it. If they do now, I know it was you."

"And you'll nobble me or wallop me," whispered Simon.

"You've got it. You're at the same school, aren't you?"

Simon nearly toppled over with surprise into the canal. He'd been sick with worry about this boy and his thuggish friends for ages. Norman and his friends had wormed their way into his nightmares. He'd been sick with worry about getting bullied by them. He imagined them stalking him, hunting him down like the beast in Lord of the Flies. He'd shed tears over them night and day, lost his joy of life and become thoroughly miserable. Yet Norman did not even know who he was, let alone his name, let alone again whether he was at the same school. How did his fishy mind work? Did he bully and punch without seeing a face? Was he totally trapped in a world of his own with no windows to the outside? How was this possible? Simon had no idea. He nodded. If he kept nodding, his head would fall off.

"Yes. You're Norman."

"How d'you know that?" Norman asked. "Guess I'm famous."

Was that it? Did he leave a trail of unhappiness and

misery behind him just to be well known? Just so that people would talk about him?

Simon had no time to think this through. Norman was explaining to him the finer points of fishing. Simon did his best to pay attention, mainly because he was always interested in learning new things. His interest, however, was blunted by fear. Norman might be being instructive, but he was still the same thug. Maybe every thug had a gentler side, or a side that took over for a few minutes when the monstrous bit rested, and when there was no one around to witness the weakness. That was what this probably was. There wasn't an audience so Norman didn't have to act big, tough and cruel. He was doing what he wanted, and judging from the black eye, needed some recovery time of his own.

"You do it," he said gruffly.

"Do what?" Simon asked.

"Cast, you idiot," said Norman.

"I'm not an idiot."

"Just do it. Go on, hold the rod, cast it."

Simon made a complete mess of it and ended up with the hook in his hair.

Norman laughed. It was the strangest sound Simon had ever heard. He wanted to laugh too but didn't know whether he should. It wasn't necessarily a kind laugh.

"You're a real little twit, aren't you," said Norman. "Here, try again."

Simon, for all of his thirteen years, could almost hear Norman's family talking to him in the same way. 'Twit, idiot, nobble, wallop'. They were words his parents would never use in a million years yet Norman probably heard them every day.

He tried three times and on the third time got it right. The hook landed in the water and Norman took back the rod. Simon stood there, silent as the proverbial lamb, still scared, but not as much as before, yet aware they were far from friends. In fact, he was increasingly uncomfortable with the situation. What was he supposed to do, or more important, to be? What purpose was he to all powerful Norman who could turn violent any second, thump him, punch him, shake him to pieces, swear at him and immediately forget him, totally and utterly? Despite being taught how to fish and shown a modicum of humanity, Simon feared for his life. It was heading towards twilight and they were alone, he and his arch enemy Norman Fell, in this wilderness out of sight of all, and beyond rescue.

"None of my family fish," said Norman. "I taught myself."

"How?" Simon asked.

"Books, stupid," Norman replied. "I can read, you know."

"I'm not stupid," whispered Simon.

"Well, it was a stupid question. I learned everything myself. My dad and my brothers, they couldn't do it, never. They ain't patient enough."

Simon was scared to ask another question in case Norman insulted again, or worse, got totally fed up with him and tossed him into the canal. But he wasn't stupid, no matter what Norman said, and started to tell Norman about different kinds of fish, where they could be found and how many of them were in danger.

"That's rubbish," interrupted Norman, "about fish being in danger. There are millions of them. Look how many oceans there are. Way more fish than people. And I know all the stuff you told me anyway."

Simon suspected that Norman didn't know 'all the stuff' he knew but he didn't say so, which was just as well because Norman really did know a lot. He went on about the different species in various rivers at different times of year, where they spawned, the best times of the year to catch them, even the best time of day, the best bait, the best rods, the largest catches and the best fishermen in the country. Simon was taken aback. Here was a surprise. His arch enemy, the brainless bully, knew more than he did, at least in this one subject. But Simon knew more about everything else. Norman, though, didn't care how much Simon knew. He cared only about what he knew, and thought himself pretty clever.

"I remember you now," Norman said suddenly. "You don't fight back, do you?"

"You're twice as big as me," said Simon.

"Don't matter. I'd fight back."

"Did you fight whoever gave you that black eye?"

Norman put his hand to his eye, winced, and told Simon to keep his mouth shut.

"You can't ask me questions then tell me to keep my mouth shut," said Simon, "that doesn't make sense."

Norman felt something tug at the rod and he immediately switched off the conversation and focused on reeling in whatever he'd caught. Simon watched, transfixed. Norman was certainly skilled, knowing when to pull, when to release, when to tug, when to loose. In the end, it was only a small fish which Norman inspected, then threw back into the water. It swam away, almost as quickly as Simon wanted to get away.

"You didn't kill it," he observed.

"Course not, dummy. Don't you know anything?"

Once more, Simon felt his hackles rising. He was so tired of these insults. He wanted to say, 'You're the ignoramus. You're a bully and an ignoramus' but here was Norman telling him instead that he was the dolt.

"I know a lot," said Simon, but it sounded rather pathetic.

"Goody, goody, that's what you are," said Norman.

Simon called to mind The Dilly Ghost. What would she say if she saw him talking to the enemy, or rather being talked to like he was the stupid one. Everything in his head was getting into a mess. Things weren't so clearly black and white, good and bad as he wanted them to be. Things he knew for certain weren't certain at all. Was this tall boy truly wicked? Could a truly wicked person teach himself to fish, then throw back the fish he'd caught into the water? Could Simon, heaven forbid, end up friends with him? He didn't like the idea much, especially if Norman insisted on calling him names.

"I'm going home now," Simon said.

Norman had fallen silent. He didn't even turn his head. Simon had vanished from his consciousness. Simon desperately needed the Dilly ghost to help. If he walked away, something would be lost for ever. He didn't know what it was but he had to try and find it. Come on, Dilly ghost, help me!

"I said I'm going," he repeated.

Norman had turned off completely. Simon had suddenly become nothing, a noise in the background, a buzzing fly, something too small even to swat away.

Simon started to walk but stopped. He couldn't leave, not like this. He had to assert himself somehow, but how. How?

"I know you can hear me," he said. "What you do is wrong. I'm not scared of you, even if you say I am, I'm not, even if you're bigger and stronger."

Norman turned his head slowly, as if the sounds had come from a thousand miles away. He turned eyes as cold as ice on Simon and said, "Twat."

Simon turned away and took a step towards home and safety. Then he heard the Dilly ghost's voice, not for real, but in his memory. She was a good friend, a weird one but still a supportive friend. She wanted the best for him. She would never call him stupid or a twat or hurt his feelings or insult him in any way. She seemed kind. She had the same problems, of being in a new space and not quite fitting in, yet she had time for him. She had probably appeared just for him, for nobody else. What should she want him to do now? She would want him to do whatever felt right, not necessarily whatever was safest.

Simon was the least violent boy of his year, and most other years. He'd never been in a scrap, never wanted to hurt anyone, never wanted to give way to anger. But here he was, faced with a bully who, for all his fishing skills and moments of humanity, still treated him as – well, someone to be pushed around and hurt in all kinds of ways, freely and without punishment. That wasn't right, and Simon could find no words to put it all right.

He turned, and without thinking or planning, launched himself at Norman, all the anger and frustration from months of torment taking shape in a hail of blows.

Norman fell off his seat, dropping the fishing rod, looking at his assailant with surprised eyes. The only people who had ever hit him were his father and his brothers, and he never fought back with them. He didn't quite know what to do. It took a few moments to realise that the boys' punches and kicks were actually hurting, so he tried to push him off and immediately slid further down the slope to the canal. If he wasn't careful...

There was a loud splash as both of them rolled over the edge of the bank, into the dark, dirty water below.

How he did it, Simon never knew, but he held on to a thick root poking out of the bank, keeping his head above the surface. Next to him, Norman was thrashing about, unable to find purchase. He had been yelling abuse after abuse at Simon but all that stopped as he realised that he was in danger.

The canal was surprisingly deep. Even in bright daylight it was often difficult to see the bed, and in the dusk, with all the dirt their disturbance had caused, it was impossible.

Simon could not even feel his feet touch earth. Neither could Norman, and he was much taller.

Simon held on to the root for dear life. All kinds of funny thoughts went through his head, whether his parents would be upset when he came home wet and bedraggled, or if they would be angry because he'd died without saying goodbye. He felt the cold and sogginess seeping through his trousers and his shirt. Still angry and shocked, he heaved himself up, scrabbling on bits of root and branch sticking out of the bank. Somehow, he pulled himself onto the ground, belly and face down, staring into the depths, watching the nightmare of Norman Fell thrashing around silently, unable to climb free.

Simon stood, looked around and picked up the longest bramble he could find. It tore at his fingers and drew blood, but he did not care. He held it in both hands, shoving the far end out to Norman.

"Hold it, hold it!" Simon yelled. "Hold the stick! Hold it tight. There's footholds on the side over here. Hold it! That's it!"

There was fear in Norman's eyes, a terrible, hollow fear. He was swallowing the filthy water, splashing madly, aware that as tall as he was, the canal was deeper, and that he could not swim. All the anger that had raged inside him for the fifteen years of his life so far suddenly vanished. Fear had quashed it. He didn't know if he would ever feel anything again. He was nothing, a boy in the dark waters, alone and scared, about to fall into absolute, endless darkness.

He felt something smack against his head. Wood, leaves and prickles. He grabbed it. He heard a distant voice calling something like, "oldit, thasit oldit". He held it and felt himself being pulled towards the bank. When he found a little purchase, he grabbed the side and climbed up, spitting water and mud.

Simon stared at Norman who knelt on the bank, staring around, saying nothing. Simon thought that Norman might turn on him, hurl insults and curses, maybe even throw him into the canal, but Norman simply knelt, coughing up water and green slime. When there was no more to cough up, he stood, packed together whatever he could find of his fishing gear, turned towards home and walked away. Not a word. Not a single word. No curse, no insult, no thanks, nothing, as if Simon wasn't there.

Simon watched him go, stunned by all that had happened, but knowing that things had changed forever. He did not know how he knew, but he was sure. He would no longer be bullied and would no longer be scared. He was Simon Roberts and he had his whole life in front of him.

0000 1111: WHIRLPOOL

The Headmistress was speaking to the entire school after the death of the queen. Dilly was struggling to keep composed. She was as upset as everyone else, engulfed in the solemnity of the event. For all the young people, this was a glimpse into a vast adult world that was still beyond them in so many ways. Dilly could not help but think of Simon who she had met just after the coronation. He had talked about it so excitedly, carried away by the colour, the excitement, the hope and the pageantry, all seen on the very first televisions. What would he make of this news? Should Dilly even tell him? Would she have the chance to tell him.

Four weeks had gone by since she had last seen him. Heaven knew how he had dealt with his mother's screams, let alone with the bully boy called Norman. She wished she could go back once more, but the WiFi YpHi had remained stubbornly hidden. Was it too late now. Did this terribly sad event mark the end of something more than a glorious seventy year reign? Dilly had to admit, she felt instinctively that she would never see Simon again. She could be wrong, but that's what it felt like. He wouldn't want to know, anyway. He was carried away with the newness of the young queen and the hope in the country, he surely wouldn't want to think about the end when it was just the beginning.

Dilly would have liked to share her thoughts with Laura, but Laura had been absent for two whole weeks. Not a word. Dilly might have spoken with Miss Roberts, but she too was away because her grandfather was ill. That was also sad. There was no news in the papers about him but Dilly hoped that the man who had painted the beautiful picture was okay and that her teacher would be back soon.

Meanwhile, Dilly became firmer friends with Beth and Becky as well as with Miriam who read as much as she did and was on the same wavelength. Dilly still couldn't spill her heart to them. None of them knew about the misbehaving mobile phone nor about Simon. They would probably never know. There was no way Dilly could think of to speak about him with anyone except Laura, and Laura was AWOL.

As the Headmistress spoke, Dilly felt that her head and heart were about to explode. It was so difficult seeing the adult world grieving over their lost queen, knowing that it meant much more than any of the pupils understood, and being powerless to change the tide of history. On top of this, her own secret adventure filled her with concern. She wanted to mend everything, that was her nature, but she could mend nothing. That was what she believed. If only she knew that Simon was well, back when the queen was young, that he had found a way through.

When assembly was over, Sam tapped Dilly on the shoulder, the same Samantha who had helped her when she'd first fainted.

"Come with me a moment, Dilly."

Beth, Becky and Miriam were leaving with her and asked if they could go, too. Sam said, 'Private, ladies,' and the three of them looked on intrigued as Dilly walked on by Sam's side. Over the past few weeks, the four of them had become pretty good friends, going to the same clubs, talking about the books they were reading, moaning about the same things and gossiping about the same people. It was, for Dilly, surprisingly normal.

"You seem more settled," said Sam. She was. "Irene thinks so, too." Dilly looked puzzled. "Miss Roberts." Oh, right. "You know why she's away a few days?"

"Her grandfather is ill."

"That's right, Dilly. He's an old man and he's not at all well. The school is allowing Irene to stay there a while, but she has sent you this letter."

Sam handed Dilly a beautifully addressed envelope, something she'd not really seen before. The letters she had seen for mum were usually bills or junk mail or business. People didn't write letters any more, but then, Miss Roberts was a teacher and teachers could be old fashioned. Sam said that Dilly could take it home and read it, or sit quietly there and read it in her office. Dilly chose the latter.

Inside were two letters, one from Miss Roberts – Dilly could not think of her as 'Irene' and one from somebody else. She didn't know until she'd read the letter from her teacher first.

Dear Dilly.

Just a quick note from me. The other letter is from my grandfather to you. I know that must sound strange but he has told me a story that is even stranger. 'There are more things in heaven and Earth, Horatio' – do you know that quote, Dilly? I bet you do. It certainly reflects what Grandfather Simon has told me.

Grandfather Simon?

Dilly stopped reading and looked up. The room was empty. Sam had left her alone to read. Irene had asked Sam to leave Dilly in peace, that the letter was private and special. Sam had no idea just how special.

I'll be back as soon as possible. Grandfather would like to come with me but he is frail and I don't think that's a good idea. He wanted to meet you very much. The thought of it seemed to make him younger and excited. How strange is that. You'll have to tell me more when I return. I hope you're settling in and making friends. I know that Laura is away for a while but Sam tells me you've made other friends, which is wonderful. Laura's family is hard to reach for some reason, but we will keep trying.

Have a good read of Grandfather Simon's letter, Dilly. He spent ages and ages writing it. My goodness, I haven't seen him so motivated for a long time.

See you soon.
Your teacher
Irene Roberts

Dilly folded her teacher's letter and slipped it back into the envelope. She took out the other one, written in a shaky but clear style – not printed – quite a few sheets, flattened them on her lap and began to read, heart in mouth, wondering if the idea bubbling to the surface of her mind could possibly be true. It took less than a second to confirm.

Dilly, it's me!

Dilly gulped and felt the room spin round a little.

I was going to begin 'Dear Dilly or 'My Dear Dilly' just like the old man I've become, but I don't feel old writing to you. I feel the same as the thirteen year old boy you met all those years ago. Remember? Well, for you it's days or weeks, for me it's years. More than years, decades. A lifetime. We met just after Princess Elizabeth became Queen, and now she is gone. Ah, Dilly, I DO feel old when I think of that. It was such a shock. She was there at the start of my life and is here at the end. We will all miss her terribly, at least us oldies.

A little while ago, my darling granddaughter asked me if I had any photos of where I used to live. I didn't, but I had the picture I painted. Yes, it was me that painted it. My first painting. Well, the second if you count the other one! You know which one I mean? It's not bad, is it, even if I say so myself. I gave it to her and asked who it was that wanted to see it. She told me your name and I was dumbstruck. Dilly! Irene said her name was Dilly! Could it be? I asked myself. By all the laws of science and nature, it could not be, yet I knew that it was.

Who can explain what happened. I have spent my whole life thinking about it, but I don't have an answer. All I know is that 'the Dilly ghost' appeared when I most needed it. Why was that? Did somebody or something plan it? Surely yes, but who, Dilly, who? I wonder if you know how desperate I was at that time. So alone and miserable. I feel sorry for that young boy, I truly do, and I wonder how he would have fared in life if a friend had not materialized out of the blue to show support and kindness. I bet you don't even know yourself how much that meant to me. It meant everything. When the crunch came, and it did come, Dilly, it really did, I thought of you and your faith in me and how much you were on my side and I made things right.

Dilly wondered what it was that Simon had done. She hadn't known then and didn't know now, but he had obviously done something. Absorbed, she read on.

I met Norman Fell by chance near my secret sanctuary, down by the canal. He was different by himself. He was fishing. Apparently, he went there a lot. It's quiet, a good place for thinking, and he had a lot to think about. I was scared out of my wits, Dilly. I thought he was going to throw me into the canal. You can't imagine how petrified I was, I could hardly talk. He talked, though, even showed me how to fish. I started to feel sorry for him. I wondered if we could become friends. That was the wrong thought. He was a bully and had hurt me and hurt others. You can be friends with someone like that if you do as they say and know that they can squash you when the mood takes them.

In the end, the bully in him came out and we fought. Not a proper fight because I would have lost, but we ended up in the canal. Imagine that. It was getting dark, the water was filthy, we were alone and Norman Fell could not swim.

I got to the edge and…

Dilly's heart skipped a beat. Surely, Simon did not let the boy drown?

…I pulled him out. He never said a word, no thank you, no cursing, nothing. After that, he ignored me for the time we were in school together and never troubled me again. I knew he wouldn't. This is the way bullies are. The problem is when they end up in positions of power, which happens a lot. You have to keep fighting them, one way or another.

You are probably waiting even now to return to see me again. It won't happen, my dear Dilly ghost. However you made the journey in the first place, it won't happen again. I know it because if it had happened, I would know, wouldn't I? And after my tangle with Norman Fell, I never saw you again.

We stayed there a few years, then moved and moved again. My mother outlived my father by ten years, but she was lost when he died. Women gave themselves to married life much more than they do now, I believe. She never forgot seeing you! Oh no. She started going to seances and to all kinds of peculiar events, and she never once came into my bedroom without looking around first, squinting and shaking.

I became a scientist, of sorts, though I never discovered anything spectacular. I married, had children, and my children had children, and one of them moved back to the Estate where we met and became a teacher. Miss Roberts to you. My lovely Irene. And you are there now, just as I remember you seventy years ago. For all my studies, I do not understand how this can be. I think you and I must have good angels looking after us.

It would be wonderful for me to see you again, but Dilly, I am unwell. Our marvellous queen has passed and I must tell you that I see the Other Side now myself. But I don't want you to be sad. You have your whole life in front of you. You said that you were lonely but Irene tells me that you are making friends and settling down. I knew you would. You are special, Dilly. You have to be, otherwise the angels, whoever they are, would not have selected you to help me. You have a generous heart, you are clever, loving, gentle and imaginative. You will make the best life for yourself that you can, I know it, and I've told Irene to help you. She doesn't know everything that happened. How can she? Even if I told her, she might think that I was a soppy old man. I probably am, now. Yet I still feel the boy inside me talking to you. He's there, in my head and heart.

I am quite tired now and I need to finish this so that Irene can post it. So I will disappear, just as you did.

Goodbye my Dilly ghost.
Simon Roberts

Dilly laid the letter on her lap. The room was intensely quiet so Dilly had time and space to try and take in what she had just read. This was the same beleaguered little boy she had seen just a few weeks past, the one she wanted to see again, to make sure he was alright. Whatever hump he'd had as a boy, he certainly seemed to be free of it now. She wondered, could she visit him. What would that be like? Would she recognise him? Would he recognise her? Dilly was full of questions that no one could answer. She doubted that there was anyone on Earth who could answer the main question of how this had happened in the first place.

There was a gentle tap tap tap at the door. Dilly had been

so lost in thoughts that she forgot where she was for a moment, thinking that it might be her mother. It was Sam. And behind her Dilly could see Beth, Becky and Miriam, all looking sheepish and shy.

"Finished?" Sam asked. Dilly nodded. "I brought some friends with to keep you company."

A chill ran down Dilly's spine. She did not know why. Sam and the three girls came in. Sam gestured to the girls to gather around Dilly who held the letter tightly but carefully. Did they know what was inside it? Had they come to ask questions?

"Miss Roberts called just now," said Sam. "She wanted to know if you'd read the letter."

"I have," said Dilly.

"She asked me also to bring your friends with you. She mentioned Laura, too, but Laura and her family seem to have vanished. Irene – Miss Roberts – said you should all be together."

"Is it about the Queen?" Beth asked.

"No," said Sam. "Keep her in your heart, of course, but no. Irene – Miss Roberts – asked me to tell you, Dilly, because you are no longer a child – none of you are – that her grandfather passed away yesterday. She said you would be especially upset, Dilly, and you'd want your friends around."

Dilly stared at Sam as though she had uttered unintelligible words. She had a letter in her hands from Simon – THE Simon – HER Simon. What was this horrid thing called 'Death' that was stealing people away, one after the other, famous people, unknown people, extraordinary people? How was she supposed to respond? She had just learned the most wonderful thing, the most marvellous thing, and now it was snatched away, by Death, the thief. She felt like she was being tossed around in a whirlpool, hardly able to catch her breath.

"Irene – Miss Roberts – never told us what was in the letter, Dilly," said Sam, worried by Dilly's white face and silence. "All she said was that, if you'd read it, you would be terribly upset and would need your friends here to keep you company."

"We will," said Beth.

"Oh yes, we will," said Becky.

"We all will," said Miriam, "even though none of us know what's going on."

"We like you," said Beth.

"And we're all sad about the Queen, "said Becky.

"We don't want you to be extra sad," said Miriam.

Dilly wasn't extra sad. The news upon news upon news was too much to be sad about. There came a point, even though she could not put it into words, where sad things came so thick and fast that you could not process them in normal time. Dilly felt that it would take her a lifetime to be understand this type of feeling..

"I'll be alright," she said. "I can't explain what's in the letter, though."

"We're not being nosey," said Beth. "We don't want to know. We just don't want you to be unhappy alone."

Dilly thought, a few months ago, she was entirely alone, in a new home, new city, friendless and unhappy. Now, barely the blink of an eye later, she had three friends wanting touchingly to raise her spirits because she was laid low by bad news. She had teachers almost as close as friends, a spiritual friend in the vanished Laura, and a fleeting friend in the form of Irene – Miss Roberts' grandfather. Simon. The bullied boy. The boy who needed her. The boy who had survived, lived his life and passed on.

"Shall I make you a cup of tea, Dilly? Tea and sugar always does the trick."

Sam left the four of them there. And in the time it took

for her to arrange for tea and biscuits to be brought, yet more startling news befell Dilly Paget.

0001 1111: AURAL COMMUNICATIONS

Dilly's mobile flashed into life. At such a moment, she could easily have ignored it as a distraction. She didn't. She looked at the screen. In bold, blinking green letters she saw a message from 'AURAL COMMUNICATIONS'.

"It's a scam," said Becky. "I'm always…"

"No," Dilly interrupted, "it isn't, but…"

She wondered what on Earth this company who she'd been chasing for weeks wanted, right now, at this precious moment.

She tapped the accept icon and there, unbelievably, was Laura.

"Hello Dilly. Hello Becky, Beth and Miriam."

Dilly doubted whether she would or could be as surprised and perplexed ever again. She doubted whether any future moments could be so intense. She almost laughed at the weight of it all, as if laughter were the only way to keep sane.

"Laura?"

"Yes, it's me. How are you, Dilly?"

"I'm… I'm… " she started, unable to find the right words. What if the universe suddenly caved in and a disembodied voice asked, 'How are you?'. What would you answer – 'Very well, thank you. How are you?' Courtesy even in chaos. "Where are you?" she asked.

"At home," Laura replied. "Although, not the one near you."

"Laura, what's happening? What's going on?"

Laura said, "It's complicated, but all is well, Dilly, it really is."

"It doesn't feel it," said Beth.

"No, it doesn't," said Becky.

Miriam stayed quiet, curious to understand.

"I had to help you," said Laura. "I'm not supposed to interfere, just to watch, but I had to. And I didn't do much, you did everything. I told mum and dad that I could not bear seeing you so unhappy, or Simon."

"Laura?" Dilly asked, wondering who this girl was, this friend who had been so close, so caring and so special. "Who are you? What do you mean, 'interfere'?"

"That's not easy to explain," said Laura. "I could have just vanished without seeing you again. It's happened before. Dad said I ought to leave things to sort themselves out now. You've met my dad, Dilly."

Had she? Dilly was sure that she had not met him. She'd never been to Laura's house, and Miss Roberts had never met Laura's parents either.

"I haven't, Laura, I'd remember."

"He's the one who gave you the phone, the engineer who installed all your computer equipment."

Dilly had to shift track yet again.

"But we looked for him, together, Laura! How could he be your father?"

Laura appeared abashed and said, "Sorry, Dilly, that was him. He was keeping an eye on me. I was as surprised as you to see the van. I think it was a projection rather than the real thing. Dad's good at illusions. I was upset that things weren't working out and he wanted me to know that he was there, if I needed him."

"What things, Laura? What wasn't working out?"

"This is very mysterious," said Beth.

"Isn't it ever!" said Becky.

Miriam weighed it all up quietly. Laura went on.

"Where I live, where I come from, we can see issues in the timeline. We're under instruction not to interfere but I did. I couldn't help it. Mum and dad were unhappy about it but they helped, to keep me out of trouble."

"Where do you come from?" Dilly asked, as perplexed as ever, and thinking that the answer might be Mars, the Moon or some galaxy far, far away.

"Same places as you and Simon. It keeps changing, Dilly, for years and years."

"She's from the future," said Beth.

"No way!" said Becky.

"My parents saw how unhappy I was because of you and Simon. It was unfair and wrong and I wanted to put it right. They love me and helped me, just like your mum loves you. What does she call her company?"

"Dilly Enterprises," said Dilly, trying her best to take all this in.

"My parents call theirs "AURAL Communications. After me."

"But that's…" Dilly began, then she got it. The anagram.

"I'm Laura, and I'm your friend, always will be. Like Beth said, I'm from a different time."

"Told you," said Beth.

"But I can't stay. It's not allowed."

A girl from the future. That was something to talk about, except they couldn't, not unless they wanted to be made fun of and be called cranks, or worse.

"I don't know what to say," said Dilly. "There's an awful lot happening at once."

"There is," said Laura, "but you're strong and clever and kind hearted. That's why I like you. I couldn't bear to see you so alone. Nor Simon. I persuaded dad to help. Mum wasn't sure but agreed, if I was careful. It's quite dangerous, messing about with mental and physical interspatial temporal anomalies…"

"What's that when it's at home?" asked Becky.

"Even when it's not at home," said Beth.

"Not important," said Laura. "What's important is what's always important, people. It's one of the things we've learned," she continued, like a professor, "everything stems from a First Principle which is to value life, not just your own, but others. It sounds corny doesn't it, but it's true. If you get that right, everything else works out. There's always sadness and trouble on Earth, isn't there. It's part of being here. But I thought this was too bad and wanted to put it right. I didn't break any rules, just bent them a bit. There was a connection between all of us and I saw a way to make use of it, to solve each other's problem. The science isn't that important."

"What connection?" asked Dilly

"All three of us had moved here at different times. My family had come from – well, doesn't matter, a long way away. You and Simon seventy years apart, Simon just after Queen Elizabeth's coronation and Dilly just before she died. You were both unhappy in different ways but there had to be a way to let you heal each other."

"Oh, that's so sweet!" said Beth.

"I think so, too," said Becky.

"Like a guardian angel," said Miriam. "It's wonderful. So Simon was Miss Roberts' grandfather?"

"He was," said Laura.

"How could you know him as a boy, then?" asked Becky.

"You're not listening," said Beth.

"I am," said Becky, "but it's a bit hard to understand."

Dilly didn't try to understand the science, only the bare bones of who Laura was and what she had done. Many muddled thoughts and emotions raced around her brain.

"Dilly, you aren't angry with me, are you?" Laura asked,

"I don't think so," said Dilly. "I'm not sure what I feel. Can't you come back properly and talk to us. Stay with us.

Be my friend again."

"I am your friend," said Laura, but she could not stay. There were rules in what Laura did. She'd already almost twisted some of them but things had worked out so she would be forgiven Dilly had settled and Simon had lived a good life, free of anger and regret.

"What's it like where you live, Laura?" Beth asked.

"Yes," said Becky, "is it different?"

"Very different in some ways, not so different in others," Laura replied. "Do you know binary?"

"Is it a game?" Beth asked.

"It's the way computers work," said Miriam, "ones and zeros."

"That's right," said Laura. "We've applied it to parts of atoms to make computers work faster and do wonderful things. It's called Quantum computing. My mum and dad know much more than me, but everything we are and everything we do is helped by quantum. I'm not allowed to say too much, it's against the rules, but it's changed everything, along with the First Principle."

"You're SO clever!" said Beth.

"You really are," said Becky.

"There are cleverer people than me," said Laura. "Cleverness isn't everything. Being kind is. Dilly, do you forgive me?"

"What's to forgive?"

"I didn't tell you the whole truth, did I?"

"No, but it would have scared me. It still does."

"Not scared," said Laura. "You were fairly fearless. It wasn't easy, what you did."

Dilly didn't know what to say. Her BFF was now a BFBNF and that was sad.

"Can we talk again?" Dilly asked. "Like this?"

Laura said probably not. Things had to progress normally now.

"I won't believe it after a few days," said Dilly. "It will be like a dream."

"You'll have something to keep that will prove it happened," said Laura, "apart from Simon's letter. Irene will bring it to you in a few days."

"Irene?" asked Beth.

"Miss Roberts," said Laura.

"Oooh, Irene," Beth and Becky said together.

"You won't forget this," said Laura.

"She never will," said Becky.

"We won't let her," said Beth.

There was a knock at the door and Sam poked her head around. It was strange for all of them, the teacher seeing four children occupying her office and the children not really wanting the teacher to come in. They still had a lot of questions but they would have to be answered in the fullness of time, literally.

"Girls, I'm afraid I need my office back," said Sam.

"One minute?" Dilly asked. "Please?"

Dilly looked at her new friends and with her eyes asked them to leave her alone with Laura for that one minute. They didn't mind. Or if they did, they didn't say.

"Are you alright?" Laura asked.

"I'll miss you," Dilly said.

"And I'll miss you. I knew I would, but I came anyway."

"I really do have a thousand questions," said Dilly.

"So do I!" Laura answered. "You might not believe it, but I do."

"I have to go. This is…"

"Teacher's office, yes. It's all real," Laura reassured her. "Wait to see Miss Roberts." The screen fizzled. "That's my dad," said Laura. "He says 'Hello' and hopes everything is working fine. He's put some special stuff in the computers for you and your mum. Ahead of its time. He knows what he's doing. I've got to go."

"You're fading, Laura."
"So are you. Bye Dilly."
"Bye, L…." Dilly started, then her screen went black.

EPILOGUE

A week later, Dilly was laying on her bed, holding a package wrapped in brown paper. Miss Roberts had returned that day and given it to her. She had stayed away due to 'special consideration' and looked quite worn out when she met Dilly.

"Tough days," she said to Dilly. "Losing the queen and Grandfather Simon on the same day. How is one supposed to feel? Anyway, how are you, Dilly?" Dilly said she was fine, and she was, despite all that had happened. "Grandfather was so keen to know all about you. He said he couldn't explain everything but that you would understand. Do you?"

"I think I do, miss."

"Excellent. Well, he gave me this for you. I haven't seen it but he's had it for seventy years but never showed it to me once. Said it was a secret that only you would know about."

This time Dilly didn't understand. What could it be? She got up, found a pair of scissors and cut the string. She hesitated before unwrapping the paper, thinking of Simon, wishing she could have met him again as a grown man. Wouldn't that have been strange! Little Simon, all grown up and wrinkly. She smiled to herself, but almost cried at the same time. She'd liked him so much and had felt so sorry for him. She was relieved beyond measure that he'd found a way through the bullying. For a moment, she wondered what had happened to Norman Fell, but despite Laura's First Principle, she did not care.

She sat on the edge of the bed, thinking for a few moments more about the meetings she'd had with young

Simon Roberts. She thought of the estate as it had been built after the war, how it was being rebuilt now and imagined what it might look like in however many years (centuries?) ahead when Laura and her family moved in. She could not picture it at all. Hopefully, it was less glassy and more comfy.

She opened the package, still not knowing what it might be, but as soon as it was revealed, she could not understand how she hadn't guessed. It was so obvious.

Inside was a framed water colour painting of a half visible girl, the mirror image of Dilly, with green eyes, curly hair and an inquisitive, shy expression, a ghostly presence through which you could see a boy's typical bedroom clutter, a fish tank with two perky goldfish and books, lots and lots of books.

THE END

Colour Your Reading

8 to 12:	Green
YA:	Red
Adult:	Magenta
Poetry:	Blue
Non-Fiction:	Gold

Hawkwood Books 2023